Social Studies
Book Two

Shattered
and Broken
plus eleven

An anthology of Short Stories focusing on Social Issues

Audrey Austin

SOCIAL STUDIES

Book Two – Shattered and Broken Plus Eleven

Also for your reading pleasure:

Book One – Dying To Be Popular Plus Eleven

Book Three – Weaving Alice Plus Eleven

A Trilogy of Anthologies

Short Stories

Which keep the focus on

Social Issues

Written and compiled by

Audrey Austin

SOCIAL STUDIES – BOOK TWO

Copyright March 4, 2014 Registration # 1111507
Audrey Austin

This is Book Two of a trilogy of anthologies containing short stories focused on Social Issues.

Cover design by Susan Ruby K.; Yuneekpix.com

ISBN 978-0-9780238-9-8

TABLE OF CONTENTS

SHATTERED AND BROKEN

"Let that be a lesson to you, bitch!" His slap on my mother's face reverberated throughout her body. Its echo made me recoil within the safety of her womb. Then I heard a door slam. Through her sobs she reassured me, "It's okay, Alicia. We don't need him anyway. I will always take good care of you, my baby." I felt the comfort of her fingers' pat, pat, pat on her tummy. Feeling safe and warm, I went back to sleep.

When I woke up it was to hear soft sounds coming from my father. He was crying. "I didn't mean it, Barbara. I'm sorry. I'm so damn sorry. You know I didn't mean it. Forgive me, babe. I give you my word I'll never hurt you again. "

My mother was crying. From where I was deep within her womb I could sense how much she wanted to believe him. I had earlier heard her telling her friend, Karen, "It will be so hard to raise Alicia on my own. If only Brandon would just grow up and get his life together. He gets so nasty when he drinks too much beer and smokes that weed. I'm scared to trust him, Karen. But I'm more scared to raise this baby alone."

"You know I love you," I could hear my father saying. "Marry me, Barbara. Our baby needs two parents. You don't want to raise a kid on your own."

I felt the fear and hesitation in my mother's voice. I began to kick as hard as I could. *Don't marry him!* I wanted to yell. I know my mother felt my kicking because I heard her say, "Give me your hand, Brandon. Do you feel that?"

"I do," he answered.

"Alicia needs good parents. I want her to have the best."

"I swear I'll be a good dad to Alicia. Barbara, will you marry me?"

She did. I tried to warn her against marrying my Dad but my kicking had the opposite effect. My Mom carried me down that church aisle and I heard them exchange their vows to love and honour each other forever.

I prayed everything would be okay and it was. But not for long.

Two months before I was scheduled to make my first appearance on earth I awakened to the sound of loud laughter. It wasn't the first time I'd heard these frightening noises.

This time Mom was rubbing her stomach. The slow movement of her hand back and forth, back and forth, helped a little to make me feel relaxed. When she raised her voice and started yelling is when I got really scared.

"Not again! Out!" she screamed. "Get out of my house you drunken bums!"

"Who you callin' drunken bums? Bitch! You talk to my friends that way?" Daddy's questions were a threat.

Whack!

The comfort of Mommy's hand left her stomach as she raised it to her stinging cheek.

"Hey man, take it easy!" I heard a strange male voice shout.

"Mind your damn business!" Daddy replied.

Whack!

I felt the punch to her swollen stomach. I could feel Mommy's body squish my own as she landed hard on the floor.

"Not with the belt man! Are you nuts?" Another strange voice yelled.

Whack! Whack!

The strangers pulled Daddy away from Mommy. They pushed and dragged him out of the house.

I lay on the floor with my Mommy. Something was very wrong. Her body was heaving with sobs and I could feel strange movement too. That's when I knew it was time for me to leave the womb. Contractions started.

Mom tried to stand up. She managed to lift herself from the floor. Pain pushed her to the telephone where she dialed 911.

I was born in the hospital a few hours later. Because I arrived two months early they kept me in an incubator for some time. Mommy had to go home from hospital without me.

"I'll bring you home soon, Alicia," she promised. I knew she was telling the truth. There was no doubt in my mind that my Mom loved me.

I missed her while I was in the incubator but the doctors and nurses treated me with kid gloves. I grew strong under their cautious care.

I was more than a month old when my parents came to the hospital to take me home with them. Dad drove the pick-up truck. Mom sat beside him and held me close to her heart. I was warmly wrapped in a blanket and as I listened to the cheerful bantering between my parents on the drive home I was hopeful that everything would be okay after all.

My mother, Barbara, was nineteen years old when I was born. Her parents had been killed in a car crash leaving her an orphan when she was just sixteen. I'd overheard her telling her friend, Karen, "It was Dad's fault. He'd been drinking and never should have been driving that night."

I was in tune with my mother's thoughts and feelings. I knew she had loved her mother and missed her very much. I also knew she felt guilty when her father died because she felt a sense of relief knowing he would not abuse her mother again.

Mommy grew up listening to the tears and shame her mother experienced at the hands of her drunken, raging father. I knew my Mom wanted me to have a more peaceful, secure childhood than she had experienced. Mom had to drop out of school when her parents died. She found a job as a waitress in our small town restaurant and that's where she met my Daddy.

My father, Brandon, wasn't much older than my mother. Unlike her, he had graduated high school and become a car mechanic. He was good with fixing things but when my Daddy was drunk he was better at breaking stuff.

Daddy learned this behaviour from his mother. My grandma on my Daddy's side liked her beer too much. Daddy grew up learning how to duck fast when his mother sailed the frying pan across the room. I heard my Mom tell her friend, Karen, "Brandon's Dad was a meek, fearful little man. Brandon told me he grew up listening to his father's *yes dears* and wanted to punch his Dad in the face for not protecting him from his mother's raging flyers.

My parents both grew up in violent homes. Even before I was born I knew I would suffer the same fate.

I hoped I was wrong when for the first year of my life our household was a peaceful one. Each day Daddy went to work in the garage. Each day Mommy fed me, dressed me, held me and loved me. I learned to take my first steps and I loved the way my parents laughed with joy when I learned to say my words aloud.

My little bedroom was next to my parents' room in our small house. It was when I was nearly two years old that it happened. I heard Mommy say, "I'm pregnant again, Brandon."

"Shit!" was all I heard my father say before he left the house slamming the door behind him.

I learned a new word that night. "Shit, shit, shit!" I laughed and repeated.

"No, no, Alicia!" Mommy reprimanded. "That's a bad word. Don't let me hear you say that bad word again!"

I was my father's daughter. "Shit, shit!" I giggled.

Mommy couldn't help but laugh. "You are just too cute for words," she said. "But I mean what I say, Alicia. No more nasty words!"

Daddy broke his promise of sobriety. He came home drunk that night. I was awakened from a sound sleep when I heard my Mommy crying, "No, Brandon. Stop it! You're too rough! You'll hurt the baby."

"Shut up, bitch!"

"Bitch, bitch!" I muttered as I lay in my crib. "Shit! Bitch!"

I was nearly three years old when I heard my Mom tell her friend, "I lost the baby because of his violence. I have to leave him, Karen. Life with Brandon is pure hell."

I watched as Mommy showed her friend the black and blue marks on her arms and her breasts. "He calls it love-making, Karen. He's become a drunken sadist!"

That afternoon Mommy bundled me up, lifted me into my stroller and, suitcase in one hand, with the other she pushed the stroller away from our house. She gave me a very long ride that day.

Then, "Mommy, I have to pee."

That's when she started to cry. Tears covered my Mom's face like a blanket. I cried too. "Mommy, I have to pee!"

The stroller stopped moving. Mommy came around and kneeling down in front of me she said, "I'm sorry, Alicia. I'm so very sorry, baby. I have nowhere to go! I'll take you home now. Can you hold it for a little longer?"

"Yes, Mommy." It was hard to hold it that long. Mommy didn't punish me when I wet my pants.

"It's okay, Alicia. We'll soon be home and I'll get you into some dry clothes."

By the time I was old enough to start kindergarten I had grown used to my Daddy's rage and my Mommy's tears. Too many nights I would lie in my bed in my little room next to my parents' room. I would hear the ugly sounds. Slap! Whack! Smack! I knew when Mommy's bruised body hit the floor. Thud!

I lay frozen in my bed. I felt guilty. I should help my Mommy but I was only five and not very big for my age. Daddy was a lot bigger than me. How could I stop him? I wanted to save my Mommy but I didn't know how.

Daddy was always out of the house when I would wake up for school mornings. He would be at work in the mechanics' garage. Mommy would always make me a good breakfast even when she was in pain. She covered the cuts and bruises by wearing slacks and long-sleeved tops but she couldn't hide the black eyes and though she took to wearing scarves she was not always successful in hiding the welts on her neck.

By the time I was ten years old my little girl's body was beginning to show changes. I was developing little breasts already. I worried so much about my Mom and the cruel treatment she suffered at the hands of my Dad. I found that eating more than I really needed helped to make me worry a little less. It never occurred to me to tell my teacher or my friends what was going on under the shameful roof of our house. I learned that eating was a comfort and I learned that eating helped me to bury my fear. Like a good little girl I learned to keep the shameful family secrets.

Because my Mommy loved me she let me eat all the cookies, sweets and ice cream I wanted. Because I ate too much I grew fat. Kids at school teased me and some of the boys bullied me. I expected that from boys. I was only ten but I had known for a long time that bullying boys grew into frightening fathers who bullied their wives.

By the time I was eleven I had the body of an overweight woman. That's when I noticed Daddy looking at me in a different way. Until then he had mostly just ignored me. He never hit me or yelled at me. It was just my mother he beat up and abused.

That changed when I was eleven.

I was in my bed one night trying to sleep. Sleep evaded me because of the racket coming from my parents' bedroom. Crunch! Mommy's cries came to a halt.

"Whore!" Daddy shouted.

I heard no further sound from my mother. Was she dead? Should I do something? Should I call the police?

Then I had no more time to consider my options. My bedroom door opened. Daddy's huge, intoxicated frame filled the doorway.

"Your useless bitch of a mother is asleep!" he said softly as his bare feet creaked across the floor of my room. He sat on the side of my bed.

I curled myself into a ball. I tried to become small. I tried to disappear. But my fat body betrayed me. Daddy's hands roamed. He did not hit me. He did not hurt me. But I wanted to die.

Daddy visited my room often after that first night.

I wanted to tell Mommy but she suffered so much already. I didn't want to worry her more than she already did. From my earliest days I had learned to keep shameful secrets. I really did not know what I could do to help myself. I buried my essence. I buried my self with food. The more I was abused by my father the more food I would eat. I was totally caught up in a cycle of shame.

Everything changed when I was thirteen.

Daddy came into my room as he often did. "Your Mom's asleep," he muttered as rough mechanic's hands did as they wished.

But this night he was not content with touching. This time he forced my thighs apart. He forced himself inside and contaminated the purity of my body.

My silent tears swore vengeance.

Then my poor, bruised mother was there. She crept into my room. I saw her arm outstretched and the knife in her hand gleamed. She plunged that knife into his back. My father's body crashed down upon me. His weight was smothering me. My mother plunged the knife again and again. "Bastard! Bloody bastard!" she shouted.

I felt my father's warm blood drip down the sides of my fat body.

My father's dead bulk pinned me in place. I could not move.

My dear mother pushed him off me. He landed on the floor beside my bed with a thud.

"I'm so sorry, Alicia. I'm so sorry," my mother cried.

My mother was found guilty of murder. She is in jail now and will be there for some time to come. I did not attend my father's funeral. I didn't want to ever be near to him again. They put me into a foster home.

I turned fifteen this year. I don't like living in a foster home but I have no choice. I dream of turning eighteen so that I can get my own place. My foster mother is a kind lady. She's mostly kept busy though looking after her own children. I know they took me in only because they can use the extra money they get from the province. My foster father is good to his own kids. He's kind to his wife.

He hasn't touched me. He hasn't hurt me. But lately he has taken to looking at me in a familiar way. I think about telling the social worker but old habits are hard to change. I just eat a lot; try to get along as best I can. I don't like the way he looks at me. I know it won't be long before he does more than look. I hope no one dies.

As for me, I'm dead already. The more I try to disappear the fatter I become. I don't know any more who I am but my mother named me before I was born. I looked it up and discovered that the name Alicia means *of noble birth*. My mother loved me. I know she wanted to break the cycle of abuse. I want that too but I feel shattered and beaten.

I've written my story. Now that you've read it, can you help me? My name is Alicia. And I'm not the only one.

PASSION FOR STAYING PUT

In a dimly lit corner of the sitting room Arthur sits, book in hand. His long, string bean body is stretched out in an old, faded lazy-boy chair that used to be maroon but now borders on a shabby pink. "Turn the lamp on. You'll ruin your eyes trying to read in this light! Storm's coming!" I send the double warning his way but he demonstrates his usual selective hearing.

Arthur Fletcher pays me not the slightest mind. I cross the room and turn the lamp on. When I approach him I watch as he raises his right hand and with a quick jig of his index finger he pushes his eyeglasses into a more comfortable ridge atop his bulbous nose. "Nothing wrong with my eyes, mother."

"If there isn't, there soon will be! And I'm not your mother!"

"Now that is a fact. My mother knew how to keep quiet when a fellow was trying to read. I'm smart enough to know that."

"Every man is smart until he says something! And you better watch what you're saying if you want supper on the table tonight."

"With a sigh he lays his book aside. I'm just joshing with you, Marion but I confess you are very proficient at getting on my nerves. Woman, don't you know you are getting me all riled up? You keep talking away while you know darn well I'm trying to read. What's the matter with you today, Marion? You're as jumpy as a virgin at a prison rodeo."

"You mind your tongue!" I snap.

I turn my back on my husband and walk over to stand before the living room's large picture window. The pounding in my head gives way to a pulsing ache.

I take a deep breath in an effort to still my mind. At last I am quiet with the view from my window.

My vacant stare barely takes in the green grass or the branches of the Maple tree as they bend in a breeze that I can tell is determined to become a strong wind. The sky is black. I don't want to look at its anger. I want release from my own.

I keep my eyes focused on the Maple standing tall on the front lawn between our house and the country road. I don't want to remember the road and I'm glad I can't see it from here. And I don't want to remember the swing that used to hang from the Maple's strong, inviting, outstretched limb. Instead I allow my mind to drift back to a better time when life was worth living; when my life held meaning and its name was Jennifer.

I wasn't always a somber soul. Yes, there was a time when I even possessed a sense of humour but that was a lifetime ago. I hold on to a vague recollection of a time when I found myself not only able but also willing to laugh at Arthur's corny jokes and nonsensical sayings. I remember a day eleven years ago when Jenny's sweet laughter filled this tiny living room.

Arthur often repeats it is time to forget. Maybe it is. Maybe he is right but I know I never will forget no matter what he has to say about it. Does he think I can fold up my memories like he rolls up the sleeves of his shirt on a hot day?

You need to move on, Marion, he says. If he has said that to me once he has said it a million times over the years. Move on? What does he know about moving on? Arthur has a passion for staying put. Any other passions he may pride himself on exist entirely in his vivid imagination which is as fictional as the books he loses himself in day after day ever since – ever since.

I stand by the window and I can still hear the lyrical lilt of Jenny's voice as she begs and cajoles her father until he gives in to her wishes. The way she can wind him around her little finger always remains a mystery to me, her mother.

Yes, I remember that day when my Jennifer asks the fatal question. "My birthday is next week daddy. You know how much I want a new bike. You will get me a new bike, won't you please daddy; pretty pretty please?"

"You know money's tight right now, Jenny. Do you think I can take a ball of steel wool and make you a bike?" Arthur answers.

"Bet you can if you set your mind to it," Jenny laughs.

Jennifer, my lovely Jenny.

As each day passes into the next it becomes a little easier to remember Jenny without succumbing to the tsunami tears that threaten to drown the past. The doctor assures me that crying is an important part of the healing process that will help me to forget. When he said that to me I resolved to keep my tears at bay. I do not want to forget and I never will.

The day Jenny left this house is the day anger moved into my heart. Now eleven years later it remains hard as steel. Since that day I belong nowhere; not in my home, not in my small country community, and definitely not in my marriage to Jenny's father with whom I choose to share nothing of my true inner feelings. I am not a singer like my lyrical Jenny but if I were I'd be a bass in a soprano world. I don't fit anywhere anymore.

I am alone. Yes, Arthur takes up space in the house but rest assured there is no room for him in my heart. I am more apt to make a rod and whip my own back than I am to confide my thoughts and my fears with Arthur. Somewhere way down deep within me the pain is screaming, *hold me Arthur. Hold me close and bring my baby home.*

But I don't say these words aloud. No, instead I turn away from the window and I say, "Look at that sky, Arthur. It's getting to be as black as a coal pit!

"Don't want to look at the sky, Marion. I'm trying to read my book and you don't need to be looking at me like that."

"Looking at you like what? I'm not looking at you at all. Why on God's good earth would I want to waste my time looking at you? I've lots better things to be looking at, thank you very much."

"I see you peeking at me through the corner of your eye."

"You see what you want to see just like you hear what you want to hear! You never listen to anything I say anyway and it wouldn't do you any harm at all to pay some attention to an old broom who knows a dirty corner when she sees one. What's that you're reading anyway?"

"You don't need to be worrying about what I'm reading. What's wrong with you today anyway that you can't leave a man alone long enough to sit and read a book?"

"Nothing is wrong with me. Why do you always have to think there is something wrong with me?"

"You have this habit of standing there ramrod straight, your eyes piercing me, Marion."

"You read too many books," I say.

"It scares me to see you all straight up like a stick of gum. Have you forgotten how to bend? Maybe you better not anyway because I'm sure if you do you're so brittle you will break in half. You're always mad, Marion. What's a man supposed to do?"

"Do? What have you ever done about anything? Stop asking what's wrong with me. Stop before I have your guts for garters!"

I can see that my sarcasm punches him in the stomach. He bends forward and rubs his tummy now before he asks, "Why are you threatening me, woman? You say there's nothing wrong with you but it's all wrong with me, is that your story? Everything is my fault? Everything is always my fault!"

"You're the one that bought the bike!"

And there it sits again like an elephant on the coffee table.

The cake sat on that very same coffee table.

"Happy birthday, Jennifer! Hard to believe you're a teenager now," I shout as I pass her my gift.

She takes her time opening the present, untying the ribbon then carefully unsticking the scotch tape at the corners of the folded paper. "Oh, Mom, it is lovely," she exclaims as she lifts the soft blue chambray dress from its wrapping.

"Stand and hold it up against you, Jen, while I snap a picture with my camera." I'm as excited as she is. My baby is thirteen years old today; not a baby anymore but my baby forever.

Arthur wheels the bright red bicycle into the living-room. "Oh, daddy, daddy, thank you. Thank you. I knew you would. I just knew you wouldn't forget!"

The chambray dress is tossed aside. "Can I ride it now?"

"Jenny, we haven't had any birthday cake yet. Don't you want to have some of the cake I baked for you before you try out your new bike?"

"Can't I ride my bike first, Mom? Just a short run! Please, daddy. Pretty, pretty please!"

"I think it's going to rain, Jenny. The sky is getting blacker than a moonless night and it's only two in the afternoon."

"Oh, let her go, Marion!"

Let her go?

I turn my back on Arthur and stare out again at the menacing sky. Wrapping my arms around myself I shudder when the first lightning bolt streaks across the blackness. "It's raining, Arthur."

"We've a good roof on the house. We're safe and dry in here, Marion."

His statement reminds me to run around the house to check the windows. Once I am assured they are all closed I return to the living-room. Arthur remains immersed in his book.

I sit in my armchair and try to relax. I don't like thunder storms. "It's teaming now Arthur." I say. I listen to the rain slapping the window. I hear the rolling thunder. I see the bright lightning forking its way to the earth. "It's not just flash lightning. It's a wicked bad storm. Arthur, did you remember to put the patio cushions away in the deck box?"

He raises his head from his book. He sits in silence.

"Answer me, Arthur! For heaven's sakes did you put the patio cushions away in the deck box?"

"Don't get so excited, Marion. Give me a chance. I'm thinking about it. I can't remember if I did or not."

"Well, if you didn't I wish you would."

"You want me to go out into the storm to put soaking wet cushions into the deck box? My sailing days are over, mother!" he laughs trying to make a joke in his usual manner.

"Ha! I've wrung more water out of my mitts than you ever sailed over! And I'm not your mother!"

"A little bit of water isn't going to hurt anything. Relax, Marion, and let me read my book."

"You should have put the cushions away. With this black sky you knew it was going to rain."

You knew it was going to rain!

I said, "I told you it was going to rain. With this dark sky it was inevitable. You shouldn't have let her go, Arthur!"

"It's her birthday, Marion. Did you see the excitement in her eyes when I brought the bike in? How can you say no to a kid who wants to ride her new bike for the first time?"

"I can easily say no, Arthur, but what good would it do me? You are forever over-riding any authority I try to have over the child. You are always taking away any chance I have to discipline her. You want to be her favourite. You are always stealing her away from me."

"Stealing her away from you? What kind of a darn fool statement is that, mother? You need a check-up from the neck-up!   Stealing her away from you?

Utter nonsense!"

"I speak the truth and you know it, Arthur"

"I've never stolen anything in my entire life."

"You don't even know you're doing it, Arthur. Always letting her have her own way; spoiling the girl. That's how you are stealing her away from me. You'd steal the milk out of my tea if you thought you could get away with it."

"Marion, will you relax?"

"I can't relax. I wanted her to have her birthday cake, Arthur. I wanted her to try on her pretty new Chambray dress. She could have gone for a ride on her bike after lunch if the rain hadn't started."

"The rain has started, Marion. At least the girl has had a chance to try out her new bike. We will have the cake when she returns."

"She should have been back by now. She's going to be soaking wet."

"A little bit of rain never hurt anyone, Marion."

A little bit of rain!

"A little bit of rain never hurt anyone, Arthur. Will you lay down that darn book for five minutes and take the patio cushions into the shed before they are completely saturated?"

"No rest for the wicked. I will go out in the downpour."

"Okay, Marion I will go out in the downpour if you are sure it will make you happy. Anything for a moment's peace."

"She's been gone too long, Arthur. What if she has gotten herself lost?"

"No one is ever lost on a straight road, mother."

The lightning begins to flash. The house is humbled under the thunder's roar. "Please Arthur, go out and look for her."

"Anything for a moment's peace. Even if it means I need to get drowned in a downpour."

The hour that follows is the longest hour of my life. I pace from room to room. I fret and worry. I turn the TV on then when the lightning flashes through the window I quickly turn it off again. I pick up a book that Arthur has left lying on the side table. I look at the cover and see its title is *The Call of the Wild* by Jack London. I flip the book open and read, "*He had been suddenly jerked from the heart of civilization and flung into the heart of things primordial.*"

Things primordial!

Arthur comes into the house through the front door. A police officer comes in right behind him. I feel the sudden jerk. I hear myself wailing from a faraway place.

I look at Arthur. He is drenched. He will need to change his clothes. He is dripping rain water all over my hardwood floors. I head for the kitchen to get the sponge mop and a bucket. "Are the cushions in the deck box now?" I ask.

"No, they are not. The wet cushions are now dripping all over the place in the shed. I only hope all that water doesn't rust the lawn mower"

Back in the living-room I mop up the floor. "Take off your wet shoes, Arthur, and get yourself into some dry clothes." I push hard with the mop. Back and forth, back and forth I push hard with the mop. I squeeze the sponge and watch as the water spills into the pail. Again I mop back and forth. I know that no matter how hard I scrub I cannot erase the memory of that day eleven years ago.

They come through the door together. Arthur and the policeman. They are both soaking wet.

"Sit down please, Mrs. Fletcher," the officer says.

From the deepest part of me the cry begins its journey.

I collapse into my chair. I watch as Arthur slides into his lazy-boy, his wet clothes soaking the bright maroon fabric of the chair.

"It is a hit and run accident," the officer says.

That very day I learn that the devil himself slammed his car into my Jenny's new bike and tore my little girl out of my life.

"We are pretty sure it was a drunk driver, ma'am. I'm very sorry for your loss."

The rain punches the roof. The thunder bellows. From a faraway place I hear a mother wailing. Who is that woman? Will she ever be quiet?

"What's that you said, Marion?"

"Are you becoming deaf now as well as forgetful, Arthur? I said take off your wet shoes and get yourself into some dry clothes while I finish mopping up this floor."

"Okay, mother."

I carry the mop and the bucket of water into the kitchen. I pour the dirty water into the sink; the gray water a reminder that the living-room floor needs a good clean. I am not the housekeeper I used to be. I remember saying to Jenny, "Someday you will have a home of your own, sweetheart. And when you do you will find there are times when nothing else will do but you must get down on your knees."

"On my knees to scrub the floor, Mommy?" she asks.

"Yes, child, to scrub the floor and while you're down there don't forget to pray." And she laughs and my heart is filled with the memory.

I grab the S.O.S. pad out of the frog's mouth beside the kitchen sink and with the warm water flowing from the tap I begin to scrub. Lightning flashes through the kitchen window and shines on the soap as it froths up and washes away the water dirtied by the floor. I always use a sponge mop when I clean the floors. I try to remember the last time I got down on my knees.

I put the pail and the mop away in the broom closet. Returning to the living room I see that Arthur is now dressed in clean jeans and a short sleeved shirt open at the collar. He has dried his thinning hair I see and, shoeless, he is once again stretched out in his lazy-boy chair, this time grumbling to himself.

"What are you grumbling about?" I ask.

"You've lost my page, mother!"

"Lost your page? Oh, sorry, that's right. Arthur, I was reading something about being jerked from the heart of civilization."

"I don't remember what page I was on."

"You were more than half-way through, Arthur. I can tell you that much."

Half-way through?

"I was half-way through to the end of the road when I found her, Marion. She was thrown from her bike. She lay so wet and still on the grass by the side of the road. I stayed with her until the police arrived. I didn't want to leave her but they insisted I come home. They have taken her to the morgue in the hospital back in town. I didn't want to leave her."

The officer speaks up. "I will take you both to the hospital now." he says.

The rain punches the roof. The thunder bellows. Together we sit on the back seat of the police cruiser. We go to say good-bye to our daughter.

I cannot say good-bye.

I stand once more in front of the window. The storm rages. Pellets of ice do their best to break the glass. I see Arthur reach out to turn on the lamp and continue to read. "Did you find your page, Arthur?"

In that instant the power goes off and we are plunged into darkness.

"Damn," he mutters. "I can't read in the dark."

"You read too much anyway. You are killing your eyesight. Come sit by me here on the sofa and watch the storm."

"I'm fine right where I am, mother."

"Yes, that's right. You know, Arthur, I have been thinking about many things and today while I was scrubbing the kitchen sink I had an epiphany.

His voice reaches my ear through the darkness and it has an unfamiliar comforting tone. "What is it, Marion?"

"My epiphany is that I am exactly where I need to be, Arthur. It is when I poured the dirty water down the drain that I realized how much I share your passion to stay put."

"Whatever you say, mother."

Maybe the day will come when both Arthur and I can move on. For now we need to stay where we are. Yes, I hide behind my sharp biting tongue while Arthur hides in his books. Together, while the storm continues to rage, we hide in the black silence.

NO MERCY FOR MAGDALENA

If I had listened to Mama and stayed away from the popular ones; if I had simply said no and meant what I said when *Big Katie* handed me the bottle, I would not now be standing frozen, gun in hand, in an old barn way out on the outskirts of the city. It is all I can do to keep my hand from shaking in order to keep it pointed where it needs to be; at the heart of Andreas Christakos. When I look into his eyes I see no fear. I see only mockery and amusement. He knows I won't shoot him. But do I?

Papa brought Mama to Toronto two years before I was born. I know nothing of the old ways except those I learn in our house. My father, Paulos Macaire, works as a short order cook in a Greek restaurant in East Toronto. The fact that he has lived in Greektown on Chester Avenue near The Danforth for nearly twenty years does nothing to make him more Canadian: if anything it makes him more Greek in his views. And he has strong views; especially when it comes to how much freedom a seventeen year old girl should have.

My mother, Maria, was born in Italy. She met my dad in Greece when she was on vacation there in the tiny village of Agrambela in the region of Akhaia. At that time, or so I am told, the population of Agrambela was somewhere around 200 people. Mama was there visiting with her aunt who had married a Greek. When she met my father Paulos she didn't know that his outlook on life matched the meaning of his name which is *small*.

She told me she found my father handsome and loving. Six months after their initial meeting they were married. Mama began to make a life together with a husband who, she soon learned, was a despot who used his authority in a mean and nasty manner. He was tight-fisted when it came to money and when Mama's cooking, or her cleaning, or her love-making didn't measure up to his expectations he had no hesitation in using that same tight fist to punch her in the arm or the chin or the stomach.

I later learned that my Mama's name Maria means bitter. I don't believe she was bitter when she fell in love with the handsome Paulos Macaire however by the time I came along she was beyond bitterness. She was filled with a rage that hovered just below her capacity to care what her neighbours thought of her. She kept a cap on it when in the company of others but in the home, let me just say that the punches my father landed on her often made their way to the end of my mother's wits and to the end of her arm. No, it was not my father; it was me, Magdalena Macaire, who heard her scream and felt her slap.

I am a first generation Canadian living in Greektown, in the east end of Toronto. By the time I was nine years old I began to journal. By the time I was seventeen I had filled eleven scribblers with my frustration, my anger, and my joys but mostly my doubts about ever finding true happiness. Being a witness to Papa's abuse of Mama and being recipient of it second-hand from my mother I knew nothing but violence as a way of life.

But from somewhere deep within me I knew there was something better, something more gentle, something comforting in life that could be mine if only I could one day escape, once and for all, the authoritative boundaries of my father's house.

When I was sixteen I was in grade eleven at Danforth Collegiate and Technical Institute on Greenwood Avenue in Toronto. I was an average student. I excelled at nothing really and other than my best friend *Big Katie* I had very few friends. *Big Katie's* real name is Katherine Lewis. She is the daughter of Anglo parents who arrived in Greektown when they immigrated to Canada from England. This made Katie an outsider in more ways than one. At least I had the advantage, living in that neighbourhood, to be the daughter of at least one Greek parent.

Katie earned the nickname of *Big Katie* when she started grade nine at Danforth Collegiate the same year I did. Katie stands four feet, eleven and weighs about ninety pounds when soaking wet. Thus the title *Big Katie*. Yes, she is a tiny girl; a tiny girl with a big heart. She is the best, if not my only friend.

The only thing that annoys me about Katie is her strong desire to be a part of what everyone deems the in-crowd; the clique; the kids who have all the parties; the kids whose parents can afford to buy them fast cars; the kids who would never waste their time or energy to even know that kids like Katie and I existed.

I didn't give her the nickname. The good looking and ever popular Andreas Christakos bestowed the name upon her. The other kids, both male and female, in the clique that Andreas led through the streets of Greektown, the halls of Danforth Tech and the avenues of petty crime adopted the nickname. Whether it was one Katie liked or disliked really had no bearing on the situation; the name stuck. I was probably the only person in the entire high school who did not call her *Big Katie.*

Be that as it may Katie had a big-time crush on the good looking Andreas Christakos. She called him her Greek God.

"He's a hoodlum and I wouldn't trust him as far as I could throw him, Katie," I said.

"But he is so good looking Maggie! I just wish he would look my way; just once I wish he would look my way."

"Forget about it! It's not going to happen."

"I will make it happen," she declared.

It was already a hot day though it was still early in the morning. August is the hottest month in Toronto. Katie was at my house early that day. She was there to help me to decide what to wear. It was the first day of the Food Festival. Thousands of tourists crowded themselves into our neighbourhood in order to celebrate a Taste of The Danforth; an annual celebration that lasts for two and a half days.

I chose one of my favourite dresses, a pale yellow sundress that fitted my seventeen year old curves just about right. Katie gave my choice her blessing. I couldn't lend any of my clothes to Katie as I was much taller and bigger than her. By then I was about five feet, seven inches tall. I towered over *Big Katie* but our size had no bearing on our solid friendship.

"Magdalena, this year I am determined to gain some attention from Andreas," she stated.

I looked into her big brown eyes and for a fraction of a second I believed that she would do exactly that. She was, indeed, resolved. To help her gain the attention she sought she had decided to wear a pair of short shorts and a revealing blouse cut low enough to show the soft swell of her tiny burgeoning breasts.

Satisfied with the way we looked, Katie and I were about to leave the house but my father had other ideas. Just as we walked through the front hall toward the door he shouted, "You are leaving the house looking like that?"

Papa was yelling at me but I could not help but notice his eyes rested on Katie alone.

"What's wrong with what I'm wearing?" I shot back at him. "This dress is very conservative compared to what most of my friends wear."

"Whores!" he screamed at us. "You are dressed like whores!"

My father's rage brought my mother into the foyer. "Paulos," she said in my defense, "Magdalena, she looks nice; very pretty. There's nothing wrong with her sundress. I made for her myself."

"Achh! I give up!" he yelled. "What can I expect from a daughter who has a mother like this one?"

Thanks to my mother's intervention Katie and I were able to leave the house. I didn't want to think about the situation in which I had left my mother and so I blocked it out of my mind knowing I could journal about it later. We walked the short distance to The Danforth where all the partying was carrying on. People spilled onto the street from the restaurants that lined the sidewalks while others poured into the cafes to enjoy the good food.

"Come on, Maggie," Katie laughed, "I am pretty sure I know where I can find Andreas."

I followed Katie until we came to the New York Café at the corner of Danforth and Broadview. I had forgotten that Andreas lived with his family on Broadview but Katie forgot nothing. And there he was, Katie's Greek God, the centre of attention, surrounded by his male buddies. I recognized all of them. They attended Danforth Collegiate and Technical Institute.

Katie had told me her mind was made up. She had made a decision and come hell or high water she was going to act on that decision. Before I had a chance to even say anything she sailed right up to the group of boys, ignoring all, but sidling up to Andreas Christakos. Purring like a kitten, she smiled and said, "Andreas, I've been looking everywhere for you."

I felt embarrassed for her when he looked down from his six foot two inch stance and said, "Get outa here, *Big Katie!* Whatsa matter with you?"

"Come on Katie," I called. "Don't waste your time!"

The last thing I wanted was to draw attention to myself but that's exactly what happened. Andreas looked past Katie and directly at me. "Pretty," he said.

"Love your pretty yellow dress. What's your name, baby?"

I wanted to ignore him but Katie, in her desperation to be a part of the in-crowd, decided to answer. "Her name is Magdalena but I call her Maggie," she said.

"Magdalena," he repeated. No one had ever said my name the way he did that morning. My name rolled off his tongue like honey from his dream last night. He owned it. He liked it. "Magdalena," he said again and I was surprised by the softness of his voice.

"OmorphEE!"

I was familiar enough with the Greek language to know he was saying beautiful.

Andreas Christakos strode toward me. Extending his hand he introduced himself, "Magdalena, I am Andreas Christakos at your service."

He was being very polite. It would have been rude of me to ignore his outstretched hand. We shook hands but he held my hand in his longer than necessary; long enough to send shivers through my body; long enough to make me wonder if this was how Mama felt when she first met her good looking Paulos.

"We are on our way out of the city, Magdalena. We are going to get away from this crowd of tourists and enjoy some time in the country on this beautiful summer day. Will you come with us?"

"No, thanks, Andreas."

"Oh, Maggie," Katie cried. "Please, let's go. I want to go, Maggie."

"Come on, Magdalena," Andreas coaxed. "We will have a good time, you'll see. Come on, my car's just around the corner."

I could have argued with Andreas. I could have convinced Katie not to go. But I found it impossible to ignore the two of them; not to mention the other boys who were friends with Andreas. They all wanted me to go for the ride into the country.

I followed the crowd. Yes, I did. I followed the crowd to Andreas's car. Together we all piled in. Andreas drove the car. I sat beside him and next to me on the front passenger seat sat a boy. I didn't even know his name.

In the back seat Katie sat between two boys. I didn't know them either and neither did Katie but from my place in the front seat I could hear them teasing Katie and complimenting her on her outfit.

"Oh, really?" I could hear Katie saying. "Thanks."

I knew Katie wasn't used to getting any attention from boys. For that matter, neither was I. And here we were, the two of us, alone in a fast moving car with four boys that, sure, we recognized from school but the truth is we knew none of them.

As promised Andreas drove for a long time. Soon we were way out in God's country. There were no houses around, no buildings and certainly no people. He pulled his car off the paved highway and onto a dirt road. He kept driving until he came to the front of an old dilapidated barn and that's where he stopped the car.

"Come on, let's party!" he shouted.

We all climbed out of the car. That's when one of the boys flipped the lid and opened the trunk. Then the three nameless boys began unloading the beer cases and the two large bottles.

Katie was smiling. I couldn't believe she was smiling. She was acting as though partying with these boys was the highlight of her life. As for me, I felt scared. I regretted my decision to get into the car and now I was afraid of what could happen inside this deserted barn. I had no idea where I was; no clue as to how I would ever find my own way home.

When Andreas shouted, *Let's party!* I felt I had no option but to follow him and the others into the barn. One of the boys had a radio. He turned it on and the barn was filled with good music. Katie started dancing with not one, but two of the boys. This made me nervous but Katie was obviously in her element and having a great time. Then another of the boys joined the dancing and the three boys made a circle around Katie who was giving the dance everything she had.

But then the boys weren't satisfied with dancing. They started pawing at Katie. "Take it off, *Bi*g *Katie!* Take it off."

For just a minute Katie looked at me. Shaking my head in the negative I said, "Katie, no! Don't do it, Katie!"

It seemed to me that Katie was finally coming to her senses. She stopped dancing and began walking toward me. "We want to go home now, Andreas. Please drive us home," I said.

"Hey, baby," he answered, "I haven't even seen you dance yet. Here, have a little drink. It will relax you."

"I don't want a drink," I said.

"Well, I do," Katie jumped in and taking the big bottle from Andreas she took a long, cool drink. She handed the bottle of whiskey to me. I had never tasted whiskey before but I had heard of whiskey-courage. I thought maybe if I have a drink I will find the courage to get Katie and me out of this mess.

If I had simply said no and meant what I said when *Big Katie* handed me the bottle, things would have turned out differently. But I didn't say no. Instead I accepted the bottle from her and took a drink. It tasted terrible and it burned as it travelled down my throat. At the same time I could feel it was giving me an edge I thought I needed in order to deal with Andreas and his buddies.

One of the boys shouted, "Let's see you both dance!"

"No," I shouted back.

But darned if Katie didn't start dancing again.

"Take it off, *Big Katie*! Take it off," they all cried.

The next thing I knew Katie was dancing topless while the boys pawed at her and called out filthy names.

"You too, Magdalena," Andreas ordered. "Dance with *Big Katie.*"

"No."

"Do it, bitch!" he ordered again.

"No."

Then Andreas moved up behind me. I felt something cold at the back of my neck. "I said do it, bitch. Do it or I'll shoot you."

Horrified I froze. I was not ready to dance but only God knew I was not ready to die.

"Do it!"

I felt I had no choice. I moved into the circle with Katie. I removed my pretty yellow sundress and danced topless. The boys, including Andreas, circled us and I felt their filthy hands on my body. Where is the gun, I wondered. It did not appear that Andreas was carrying it nor did it appear that one of the other boys had a gun. As I danced I looked around. Then I saw the gun lying on a shelf on the barn's wall behind where Andreas was dancing.

Without motioning or saying anything to Katie I knew what I had to do. I danced toward Andreas. I danced as provocatively as I could. I wanted to make sure that he noticed nothing and no one but me. I danced close to his tall, lean blue-jeaned body and I moved in such a way that he began to dance backward toward the wall.

"Let's be alone," I whispered in his ear.

Oh, yes, he liked my suggestion. Once we were close enough to the back wall of the barn I reached out both my arms to put them around the neck of the handsome Andreas. It wasn't difficult. I soon had the gun in my hand.

"Move it!" I shouted.

Gun in hand I ordered the boys to stand together in the centre of the barn. "Come over here, Katie," I yelled.

With Katie standing behind me it was all I could do to keep my hand from shaking in order to keep it pointed where it needed to be; at the heart of Andreas Christakos. When I looked into his eyes I saw no fear. I saw only mockery and amusement. He knows I won't shoot him. But do I?

I could see fear in the eyes of the other boys. Yes, I knew they were frightened but they didn't want to show their fear. Instead they kept up a false bravado, "Hey bitch, put the gun down. Put the gun down, baby," they all shouted.

"It's a long walk home, Magdalena," Andreas smirked.

"Stay behind me, Katie," I ordered. Then looking into the faces of these boys I suddenly saw only the face of Paulos, my father. How often had I watched him punch and kick my mother? Too often had I felt her frustration as she slapped me instead of attacking the one who caused her such grief.

I will not be like my mother, I resolved as I stood there staring at these boys. I will not be abused like my mother. I will not be harassed. I will not! I will not!

71

I heard the gun go off. I saw Andreas fall to the floor of the barn; I watched the other three boys race out of the barn. I heard the car's engine as it roared off down the dirt road toward the highway. I heard Katie's sobs. But I was frozen.

If I had listened to Mama and stayed away from the popular ones; if I had simply said no and meant what I said when *Big Katie* handed me the bottle, I would not now be standing frozen, gun in hand, in an old barn way out on the outskirts of the city. I have done the devil's deed. I have killed a boy.

Katie and I were fully dressed, huddled together on the floor of the barn when the police officers arrived. The handsome Andreas lay in a large pool of blood.

I am in jail now. I confessed to the crime. The jury listened to Katie and they listened to me as I told my story. They were not sympathetic. Katie was not charged. No, it was only me who had pulled that trigger. It was only me who now lives in a prison; a prison different from the one I grew up in with the perverted Paulos and the mean Maria.

I am alone as I write in my journal. He knew I wouldn't shoot him. If I close my eyes I can still see the mockery and the amusement he enjoyed at my expense. He thought he knew it all but I guess I showed him. Andreas Christakos knew nothing about me. I pulled the trigger and now he will never know anything again. Yes, I am alone as I write in my journal.

VALENTINE GUFFAW

School was out for the summer. Jimmy was very excited as, with the help of his father, he packed his clothes into the little brown leather suitcase that morning. He hadn't seen Grandpa since last summer. Eight year old Jimmy lived in Toronto with his parents. His mother was a dietitian and his father was a lawyer. Both were hard-working professionals.

Throughout the school year child-care for their son created no problem for the busy couple. Jimmy was in school most of the day and his mother, Anne Lincoln, was able to work her schedule around the hours he was home after school. She never needed to work on weekends although she did work hard on Saturdays catching up on the family's laundry and housework.

Jimmy never minded when his Mom was kept busy on Saturdays. He enjoyed spending time with his best friend Benny. Often on Saturday afternoons they would walk the two city blocks together to the matinee at the local movie theatre. Occasionally there were times, like during the March Break for example, when after breakfast Jimmy would leave the house in the mornings with his mother. She would head off to work and Jimmy would go in the opposite direction to the home of the next door neighbours. There he would spend his days playing with his school mate Benny until his Mom came home from work.

When Jimmy was a baby and up until he started pre-kindergarten his mother took the summer months off work and stayed at home with her son. For the past four years though, ever since his fourth birthday, summer vacation for Jimmy Lincoln meant two months of fun with his Grandma and Grandpa Lincoln who lived in a funny little farm house in the small Village of Kettleby which was less than an hour's drive north of Jimmy's home in Toronto.

This year was different though.

As he helped his son to fold and pack the shorts and T-shirts into his suitcase Mark Lincoln talked about how life had changed for Grandpa Lincoln since his wife, Jimmy's Grandma, had died and made her journey up to Heaven. "It's been almost a year now, son, since your Grandma passed away and your Grandpa has been feeling lonely. I know you will be a big help to him and good company."

"I'll miss Grandma too, Daddy. She was always there for me on my summer holidays."

"I know you will, son, but this summer I need you to do your best to cheer your Grandpa up. That's what he needs. His loneliness has made him lackadaisical. He doesn't pay as much attention to things around the house the way he did when he had your Grandma there to give him the old what-for if he didn't get his chores done."

"I'll do my best, Dad. I'll find ways to make him laugh again. I always love Grandpa's belly laugh. It's contagious. I remember when he laughed everybody laughed; even Grandma. And even Grandma if she was mad at Grandad. You remember Grandpa's great laugh, don't you, Dad?"

Mark Lincoln swiped the tear from his eye. He missed his mother. He missed his father too. Even though he lived less than an hour away his big city law practice kept him so busy that he didn't see his Dad as often as he would have liked.

To his son he said, "You bet I remember your Grandpa's laugh. I grew up there in Kettleby, don't forget. I lived there with my parents in their funny little house long before the big estates filled the Village. There were a very few houses there when I grew up. Mostly I remember the fields, the trees, the little country school and the raspberry bushes. I could spend a whole day in the woods munching on raspberries."

"I love raspberries too, Dad. Maybe I will pick some while I'm there with Grandpa, eh?"

"You'll be hard pressed to find them as easily as I did though, son. All those big expensive houses have taken up all the land where I used to run and play."

"But Grandpa still has a big backyard, Dad. If there are raspberries to be found, I'll find them."

"I'm sure you will, son."

Just then Anne Lincoln shouted up the stairs. "Are you packed yet, Jimmy? It's time to get the show on the road."

"Coming Mom."

Mark tried to close the lid on the suitcase. "Oops, looks like maybe we packed too much, son. You hop up here on the bed. I need you to sit on the top of the suitcase so I can close it tight."

"Okay, Dad."

"Jimmy! Mark, it's getting late."

Jimmy balanced himself atop the suitcase, waving his arms like a tightrope walker causing his father to laugh aloud.

Jimmy liked his father's laugh. It came straight from the belly and it was contagious. Soon they were both laughing. "Hey, Dad, you laugh just like Grandpa."

"Well, guess I could do a lot worse, son. Come on now; let's get a move on before your Mom gets mad at us."

………..

Jimmy sat in the back seat of his father's car. It didn't seem very long before the city's skyscrapers were left behind as they travelled north on Highway Eleven. There was no evidence of the farmers' fields that his Dad had told him were there in his childhood years. Instead they travelled through one town after another. They were passing through the Town of Richmond Hill when his Dad said, "Nearly there now, son."

Then to his wife, Mark said, "Should we stop somewhere for lunch before going on to Dad's place, Anne?"

"No, I think we should go straight to the house. I'll make lunch for us all when we get there. I put a couple of bags of groceries in the trunk. Lord knows Dad's cupboards probably won't be very well stocked."

"The supermarket is not far from the Village, Anne. If we find that's the case when we get there you and I can buy what's needed before we head back to the city."

"That's a good idea, Mark."

Jimmy sat quietly in the back seat listening to the conversation between his parents. It was a reminder of the shopping trips he went on in past summers with his grandparents. Grandma Lincoln was always so careful to choose foods that were healthy and *good for a growing boy* she always said.

On the other hand Grandpa Lincoln would pick up the big bag of potato chips or the chocolate chip cookies or the popsicles and ice cream bars and put them into the grocery cart. "We got to break the rules sometime," he would laugh.

"Not on my watch," Grandma would insist and as fast as Grandpa could put the good stuff into the cart she would be whipping it out again.

"I remember shopping with Grandma and Grandpa," Jimmy said to his parents. "I'm sure going to miss Grandma even if she did make me eat healthy."

"Why do you think I brought along these groceries, Jimmy? I don't want you and your Grandpa existing on TV Dinners and Kraft Dinner the whole summer," his mother responded.

"We're here," Mark announced as he swung his car right and drove along the dirt driveway which ended at the old garage beside Alfred Lincoln's country farm house.

In years past Jimmy's Grandpa Alfred would come rushing out the front door of the house to greet them when they arrived. This year was different again. This time the visiting trio crossed the verandah and stood before the front door and still there was no sign of Alfred.

"Hope the door is not locked," Mark said. He turned the knob and the three entered the house. "Dad!"

"We're here, Grandpa!" Jimmy shouted.

"He's probably asleep in his chair," Anne said.

"Dad!"

"Grandad!"

Continuing to call they made their way through the living-room and the dining room.

"Where are you, Grandpa?"

"Well, he must be upstairs." Anne declared. "Mark, I'll start putting these groceries away and start preparing lunch. You & Jimmy go wake your father and let him know we're here."

Jimmy followed his father up the stairway to his Grandpa's bedroom. He could see that the bed was sort of made but not to his Grandma's high standards. There were lots of lumps and wrinkles in the flowered top quilt. Grandpa was not in the bed. Nor was he in the reading chair. Nor was he anywhere in the bedroom.

"Dad!" Mark checked the bathroom while Jimmy ran ahead looking into the other two bedrooms. "Grandpa!"

Back in the hallway Jimmy was concerned. "Where's Grandpa, Dad?"

"Don't worry, son. He's probably out in the backyard. Let's go look, okay?"

Together they descended the stairs, passed Anne in the kitchen as she was slicing some vegetables with the intention of making a salad for their lunch and made their way into the large backyard.

They found him sitting on the summer's green grass, back against an old Oak tree, sound asleep.

Jimmy was the first to approach. He reached out and tapping on his Grandad's shoulder he quietly spoke, "Wake up, Grandad. We're here!"

Alfred hadn't meant to fall asleep. He had wanted to be there at the front door to greet his son, his daughter-in-law and his one and only favourite grandson. Now he opened his eyes and was dismayed to see that he was stretched out on the back lawn beneath the old Oak tree. "Jimmy?"

"Yes, it's me, Grandpa. Wake up!"

"Oh, I'm not asleep, my boy. Not asleep at all. Just resting my eyes," he insisted. Mark reached out his hand and helped his father to his feet.

"Hi Dad."

"Hello son. Good to see you boy. Where is your pretty wife?"

"Mom's in the house making lunch, Grandad."

"Then let's get us into the house," Alfred said.

Anne had made a delicious salad; a healthy blend of Romaine lettuce, Alfa sprouts, cubed cheddar, cherry tomatoes, mushrooms, lentils, kidney beans, and baby spinach all topped with a home-made dressing made with Lemon juice, white vinegar and savoury herbs. It filled a large bowl in the centre of the kitchen table. Also on the table was a basket filled with whole wheat dinner rolls. "And there's some frozen yoghurt in the freezer for dessert," she said. "Come on now, everybody sit down. I can't be the only one who is feeling hungry."

Jimmy sat beside his father opposite his grandfather. As he helped himself to the salad he blurted, "Sure seems funny to be here without Grandma. Grandma used to make good salads too. Do you remember, Grandpa?"

"Yep, I sure do remember. I remember lots of things. The funniest thing I can recall about your Grandma is that each year we would go to the Valentine's Dance at the Senior's Centre. Yep, Esther would put on a curly red haired wig and dress up like Lucille Ball wearing a dress covered with red hearts. She'd do a monologue that cracked me up. Now you know your Grandma was teetotal. I never knew her to take a drink ever. But she'd do a monologue pretending she was drunk as a skunk. She was Lucille Ball drunk on champagne. Yep, Esther was as funny as Lucille herself; maybe even funnier."

"And she made you laugh, Grandpa?"

"Yep, that sure did make me laugh. And speaking of home cooking, for forty-eight years that woman prepared my meals, son. That first year we were married she used to do her fair share of burning the food. She'd get so upset with herself. I'm the one that taught her how to laugh about it and the truth of the matter is the more she laughed the better the cooking."

"I sure miss Grandma but I guess you miss her more than me, Grandpa."

"Yep, I sure do, son. She laughs with the angels now and she took my laughter along with her. I can't find it inside me anymore. I'm just an old empty shell of a man now."

"I miss Mom too, Dad."

"Me too," Anne said. "She was a wonderful cook. Did you know it was Mom who taught me how to make this salad you are enjoying today? She was a wonderful teacher and always served good healthy meals."

"Have you been eating okay, Dad?" Mark asked.

"Yep, I'm okay, son. I buy those things in a frozen tray; stick 'em in the oven and that's my supper."

"Those T.V. Dinners have next to no nutrition, Dad," Anne explained. "Lots of cookbooks here in this kitchen. Why not do some real cooking?"

"You could teach me, Grandpa."

"Sure, son. Don't you worry. As long as we got peanut butter in the house we won't go hungry."

Everyone laughed but Jimmy noticed that Grandad didn't even smile. He was serious. Jimmy was glad he liked peanut butter.

After lunch Anne washed up the dishes and put them away in the cupboard. She gave the kitchen a much needed clean up while the three males sat and talked together out on the front veranda. Once her tasks were complete she joined them on the porch.

"Time to get a move on, Mark."

"Yes, okay, Anne. Now Jimmy, you have everything you need and remember, son, we are just a phone call away."

"Okay, Dad."

There were hugs all around. Alfred stood in the doorway and watched them leave. Then he closed the door and said, "It's just you and me now, son."

That evening Jimmy and Alfred spent their time together playing Hearts. Jimmy won most of the games. "I'm getting pretty good, eh, Grandpa? Usually you beat me at this game!"

"Oh, Jimmy my boy, my heart's just not in the game."

"Want to play something else then, Grandad?"

"Wouldn't make no never mind, son. One game is as good as another."

"You sure have changed a lot since the last time I saw you, Grandad."

"It's true I have. Since Esther left to meet her maker I just lost all my get-up-and-go."

"Well, where did you lose it, Grandad? Maybe I can help you find it."

"Well, my boy, if anyone can I am sure it is you."

"The Kettleby Fair starts tomorrow, doesn't it?"

"Yes, son, I believe it does."

"That means tomorrow is the parade, Grandad. Is it the same as all the other years, starting at the top of the hill then travelling west and across the bridge to the fairgrounds in Tyrwhitt Park?"

"As far as I know."

"We are going to go, aren't we, Grandad?"

"I suppose so, son. If you really want to go, I'll take you. But it will not be the same without my Esther. Nothing can ever be the same again."

"Grandpa, maybe some things will be the same. You know every year they have the parade. And all day there is entertainment up on the stage. And we can get our pictures taken together, Grandad. And maybe in the marketplace we will find something that will make you laugh again. I sure do miss hearing your big belly laugh."

"I'm sorry to disappoint you, Jimmy, but Esther took the laughter with her when she went to meet her Maker."

"Yeah, I know that Grandad. You already told me that."

"Oh, did I? Well, repeating things is just one of the things that happens when you grow old, son."

Jimmy took a good long look at his grandfather. "I never once ever thought of you as being old, Grandpa. Never once until now. I think it must have been your laughter that was keeping you young. Grandad, do you ever think of asking Grandma to send the laughter back?"

Alfred's eyes began to water. "Out of the mouths of babes," was all he said.

That night when Jimmy went to his room he knelt beside his bed and prayed, "Dear God, and you too Grandma if you can hear me. Grandpa has lost his laughter and he's awful sad. Will you please send Grandpa's belly laugh back to him? He needs it badly. Thank you and Amen."

Throughout the night Jimmy slept sound but when he awakened the following morning he had a plan for his Grandpa.

Alfred put together a breakfast of corn flakes and toast. He poured himself a cup of coffee and for Jimmy he filled a glass with milk. "The parade starts at noon, Jimmy. What do you say we leave the house around 11:30 and walk up to the top of the hill?"

"Sounds good to me, Grandad." Then, "Grandad?"

"Yep. What son?"

"Does the Bailey family still live down the street?"

"The Baileys, sure. They've been living here nearly as long as I have. Why you asking about the Baileys?"

"Oh, no special reason. Grandad, is it okay if I do a little exploring while you do up the breakfast dishes? We've got lots of time if we don't leave the house until 11:30."

"Sure, you can go for a walk but don't go too far with your explorations. I don't want to have to come looking for you."

The kitchen door slammed and Jimmy wasted no time walking down the country road toward the Bailey's farmhouse. He formulated his plan in his mind. *Should work as long as Ethel Bailey is willing to go along with it,* he decided. He felt confident that she would because, after all, Ethel Bailey had been Grandma Lincoln's best friend. Ethel answered his knock on the front door. "Well, glory be, look who's here. Hello Jimmy. My goodness, that means another year has gone by. How are you, son? Come in."

Jimmy visited with Ethel Bailey for more than an hour. When he left her house he was smiling.

Alfred climbed the hill with his grandson. They stood with the small crowd and enjoyed the passing parade. Afterward they walked over to the fair ground. There were lots of activities taking place. There was a stage set up in the park there was entertainment scheduled throughout the day.

"What time is it now, Grandpa?"

Alfred glanced at his watch. "It's just going on for one o'clock, son. I think it's time we get ourselves a couple of hotdogs, what do you say?"

While they were eating the hotdogs Jimmy said, "Grandad, I want to go over by the stage after we eat. Okay with you?"

"Sure son, whatever you want is fine with me."

They ate their hotdogs, drank the Coca Colas and after a trip to the bathroom they headed over to the stage area. There was a lot of good music. There were clowns. There were dancers and singers. There was plenty to make a man smile and even some to make a person laugh but Alfred never smiled and laughter was the last thing on his mind.

"What time is it now, Grandpa?" Jimmy asked again.

"What's your big concern about time, son? " Alfred asked but again he glanced at his watch. "It's quarter to two," he stated. "Day will soon be over."

"It's not over yet, Grandad." Jimmy crossed the fingers on both hands. It would soon be two o'clock. He hoped his plan would work.

The singing trio left the stage. The audience offered resounding applause. The Master of Ceremonies stepped back up to the microphone and announced, "Ladies and Gentlemen, our next performer has asked me to tell you that what she is about to do for you all is a tribute in memory of a dear friend of hers, Esther Lincoln."

"Esther Lincoln? Jimmy, did the fellow say Esther Lincoln?"

"He sure did, Grandpa."

The announcer continued, "Ladies and Gentlemen, I give you Miss Lucille Ball.

"Oh, my Lord," Alfred shouted.

Ethel Bailey came onto the stage. She was barely recognizable in her curly red Lucille Ball wig. It was the end of June but her costume made everyone believe it was Valentine's Day. Ethel was wearing a dress covered with red hearts. She started her monologue pretending she was drunk as a skunk. It was Esther's old routine that she used to perform at the

Senior Centre. Ethel Bailey was Lucille Ball drunk on champagne.

Jimmy prayed he didn't make a big mistake. At first he wasn't sure what he was hearing. His grandfather sort of snorted a little. Jimmy couldn't call it a real laugh. But then it happened. Ethel Bailey staggered across the stage, champagne bottle in hand. The crowd roared. And then it happened. It started way down deep in Alfred's belly and when it emerged it was a loud and boisterous guffaw. Jimmy felt as though the Heavens had opened and his Grandma had come down to Tyrwhitt Park. She gave Grandpa back his laughter. It was an answer to prayer.

"Thank you, Grandma," Jimmy whispered. For sure he and his Grandad would spend a wonderful summer together.

FRANCESCA'S CONFESSION

"Dear Rolland, There was a moment when things were somewhat placid in our lives. A moment when I thought that nothing was more beautiful, more inviting or more calming than our existence. I'm so sorry about what happened but, if this makes sense, I'm even sorrier that it didn't happen sooner…"

"Claptrap!" I shout at the TV screen. "I'm sick to death of listening to all this corny romantic babble! I can't tolerate five more minutes of this garbage! It's just drivel; a waste of air space so advertisers can pedal their detergents!" I push the off button on the remote plunging the living-room into sudden silence.

"Hey, I was watching that!" Harvey yells.

"It's crap! I don't want to watch it!" I yell back.

I turn my head and look over at Harvey wrapped in his lazy-boy chair. He's holding a bag of Smart Pop in one hand and a can of Molson's Canadian in the other. I love my Harvey but I wonder whatever happened to the good looking guy he used to be? That fellow left a long time ago and I have no idea where he went. The large lump in the chair is a sad caricature of the man I thought I was marrying.

I wonder if there's ever been a moment when things were somewhat placid in our lives. Maybe many years ago but today nothing comes to mind.

"Geez, Harvey, you're getting your popcorn all over the rug. I just vacuumed this morning. What a slob!" I shout as I bend my large body over and reach down to pick up the popcorn bits sprinkled all over my new yellow carpet.

"Francesca, you sound just like your mother; rude, crude, and offensive! I was in the middle of watching that movie so turn it back on!"

"Leave my mother out of it!" I shout. "You sit there with your beer belly hugging your knees and you've got the nerve to call me offensive? Give me a break!"

"Francesca, I'm telling you to turn the TV back on. Next time I won't be so nice about it!"

"Ha! You're all mouth! You're full of hot air! If you want the stupid TV on then turn it on yourself!" And I throw the remote control across the room. I don't know it's going to hit him in the face. It's not like I'm aiming. It's a fluke; a phenomenon, an accident! I don't mean to hurt him.

"Good gravy, woman! What have you done?"

Oh, my! What have I done? I see the blood on his face. It's dripping down his cheek just below his right eye. I pull myself out of my lazy-boy chair and nearly trip over my feet getting into the bathroom where I grab a clean facecloth out of the cupboard. I run the cloth under the warm water tap, give it a quick wring to stop the drips and then hurry back to the living room. I don't want the blood to drip onto Harvey's chair. It cost us a small fortune to have the lazy-boy chairs recovered. It was only a month ago that I had the living-room all done up and I'm not about to have him leave it in a bloody mess. I'll never be able to get blood stains out of the fabric.

"Stay still, Harvey! Let me wipe the blood off your face!"

"Be careful, woman! Take it easy! That hurts!"

"I'm sorry, Harvey."

That's when I remember the line from the old movie, *"I'm so sorry about what happened but, if this makes sense, I'm even sorrier that it didn't happen sooner..."*

"No, no, no, I don't mean it, God." I pray in silence so Harvey can't hear me. "I didn't want to hurt Harvey sooner. I really am sorry this happened at all." I bow slightly in genuflection then to Harvey I say, "Hold the cloth against your cheek. Keep the pressure on it to stop the bleeding. I'll go get a couple of band-aids out of the medicine cabinet."

In the bathroom again I grab the box of bandages out of the cupboard. I'm about to leave the room when the fat woman in the full length mirror on the back of the bathroom door stops me in my tracks. I have to admit I don't like the look of the person staring back at me. I decide Harvey can wait. The bleeding had pretty well stopped and if it hasn't he can hold the cold beer can up to his face to stop any flow. I try to remember the last time I saw Harvey without a can of beer in his hand. He sure didn't have that beer belly when I married him thirty-five years ago.

I'm transfixed by the mirror. Who am I to talk about Harvey, I think, as I stare at the sloppy woman in the mirror. Whatever happened to Francesca Fabbrini? Where did I go? One minute I'm my father's Italian princess and the next I'm Francesca Miller, wife of Harvey Miller, mother of four kids, chief cook and bottle washer for a lost tribe of ungrateful, unappreciative freeloaders. One minute I'm a devout Catholic kneeling at the foot of the cross and the next I'm a converted Jew who secretly sends her Jewish children to catechism classes. I am not a good person.

And the kids never tell on me. Harvey never finds out about my deception but I know the kids grew up confused not knowing whether they should celebrate Chanukah or Christmas. Now that they are all grown up with careers and families of their own none of them have any religion at all. Who's to blame? Me? Harvey? What did we know? We did the best we could. They are all good kids and I don't blame them if they don't visit more often. Who wants to listen to me and Harvey fighting all the time? Nobody wants to be here. I don't want to be here. I don't recognize that fat woman. Enough with the mirror!

I carry the box of band-aids out to the living-room. Harvey's face has stopped bleeding and I see that the remote's crash landing left a very minor cut on his right cheek. I take a band-aid out of the box and apply it over the cut on his face.

"It might swell up, Harvey! The bleeding's stopped but it could leave a bruise."

"Yeah, so what's your problem? You don't want to witness the results of your own abuse?"

"Abuse? You're calling me an abuser? Now, if that isn't just the limit!"

"Aah, go soak your head!" Harvey shouts. He gets up out of his chair and lunges toward me. Is he going to hit me? For the first time in more than thirty years I feel scared. Harvey raises his arm then roughly reaches out, leans down and grabs the remote that is lying unbroken on the yellow carpet beside the coffee table.

"Rolland, my dearest Rolland, will you forgive me. Can you possibly forgive the unforgivable?"

"I give up!" I shout. "What do you get out of this drivel anyway?"

"Francesca, to you everything is drivel! Shut up and let me watch my movie!"

"Who talks like that? Harvey, name me one person we know who talks like that? *Can you possibly forgive the unforgivable*? Who says stuff like that?"

"Not you, that's for sure!" Harvey bellows. "You're so perfect! You don't need to be forgiven for anything, eh? What about the time you broke the broom over my head? What about that night you poured all my beer down the toilet? What about that, eh? And what about this cut on my face? You threw the remote at me. You did it on purpose! Who does stuff like that? You! That's who does stuff like that!"

"For Pete's sakes, Harvey, to hear you talk a person would think I was a mass murderer!"

"Yeah, well, who knows what's coming next? No wonder I like these old movies. Women knew their place in those days. They knew how to hold their tongue and make a man feel good about himself; something you know nothing about. No, Francesca, you and your hot Italian temper are so perfect you never do anything that needs to be forgiven!"

"Big bag of wind! Watch your stupid movie!"

"I would if you would shut up for five minutes, Francesca!"

I leave the living-room and walk out to my sunny kitchen with the blue daisy wallpaper and the matching blue ceramic floor.   I sit at my kitchen table and think about what Harvey just said. It's true. Since marrying Harvey I never ask for forgiveness. It's his fault I don't practice my Catholic faith and it's his fault I never apologize for anything.

I try to remember the last time I said the words, *"Forgive me Father, for I have sinned."*   It was a long time ago.

And just like that I make up my mind. I'll go to confession; better late than never.

I leave the kitchen and walk past the living room door. The movie has ended at last. I see Harvey has finished eating his popcorn and has made a good start on some pretzels.

While he sits in his chair, beer can in one hand, pretzels in the other, watching the football game; I climb the stairs and go to my bedroom. I do a quick change out of my jeans and sweat shirt and climb into my best tailored suit. I kick off my scruffy slippers and become a circus acrobat getting into the unfamiliar pantyhose. I scrunch my toes into the black heels; give the shoes a quick wipe to remove the long-collected dust then make my way into the bathroom.

I pull the cosmetic bag out of the cupboard; unzip the bag and rummage around in it looking for some blush and a lipstick. As I do so I try to remember the last time I wore lipstick. Perhaps Harvey is not the only one who has let himself go?

And then I try to remember when Harvey last looked at me; I mean really looked at me and saw a woman? When is the last time he said he loved me and meant it? I should be a TV set. Maybe then Harvey would pay some attention to me. I apply pink blush and comb my hair.

At last I'm ready. I call out as I head for the front door. "I'll be back in an hour, Harvey!"

"Yeah, yeah!" he mutters.

It's a short walk to the church. I stand outside and read the words over the door, *Church of the Purification.* Yes, I'm in the right place. I'll seek forgiveness. I will be purified.

And then it's happening. I'm sitting in the confessional and I can hear my timid voice almost whispering, "*Forgive me Father for I have sinned. It has been thirty-five years since my last confession.*"

My memory isn't what it used to be and after a while I begin having some trouble remembering the error of my ways. Thirty-five years is a long time and there was definitely lots of room for error. I begin with the present and then start to work my way back. I confess throwing the remote at Harvey.

"But I didn't mean to hit him, Father. I was just venting my frustration,"

I confess that I was insincere in my conversion to Judaism.

"But, Father, how else was I going to get Harvey to marry me?"

I confess that I have a hot Italian temper and I confess that I secretly sent my Jewish children to Catholic catechism classes.

"But, Father, how could I do otherwise?"

I am in the confessional for over an hour when the priest speaks up. I hear his long drawn out sigh and then, "Mrs. Miller, are you nearly finished?"

"Well, Father," I say, "I'm back to 1985 so I still have a few years to go."

"Can we save the rest for another day, Mrs. Miller?"

"But, Father, I need forgiveness for thirty-five years full of sins."

"Mrs. Miller, you have waited thirty-five years to confess. I assure you God will understand if you wait another day to continue. Go home now and come back tomorrow."

I feel insulted but I say, "Yes, thank you, Father. I'll do that."

I'm out on the sidewalk and on my way home. I feel much better. They say confession is good for the soul and now I know that more true words cannot be said. I feel much lighter. I decide that as soon as I get home I'll apologize to Harvey for hitting him with the remote even if it was an accident.

I must have been away longer than I realized because when I enter the house the football game has been replaced by another old movie. Ignoring the dialogue I go upstairs to change back into my jeans and sweatshirt. Then downstairs again and into the living-room I'm ready to make my apology.

Harvey is still stuck in his lazy-boy chair. Ida Lupino is whispering sweet nothing garbage to somebody but I don't pay too much attention to anything except the pretzel bits and potato chips all over my new yellow carpet.

I forget all about apologizing.

"Harvey Miller! Look at the mess you've made this time! What's the matter with you anyway? Do you ever stop eating? And will you ever stop being such a slob?"

He doesn't answer back. I bend down on my knees and begin gathering the scattered chips and bits. There are too many to transport to the garbage can in my hand. I'll have to pull the vacuum cleaner out to clean up the mess.

"I swear, Harvey, you're worse than any five year old!"

Still he doesn't answer back. That's odd.

Still on my knees, I turn to look at him. All he does is watch TV, eat and sleep. He's fallen asleep in his chair. "Wake up, Harvey, for heaven's sake!"

But Harvey doesn't wake up. He doesn't move.

"Don't play games with me Harvey Miller! Wake up! Oh, my God! No, no, no! Oh, my God, no. Please don't let this be happening!"

The police listen to my confession. Unlike the priest they don't ask me to return another day. They arrest me when I tell them I hit Harvey with the remote.

"But the bleeding had stopped," I insisted. "It was just a little cut! I put a band-aid on his face. You can see that, can't you?"

But the internal bleeding had not stopped.

For a short while the police allowed my wrists to remain uncuffed while I attended Harvey's funeral. Tomorrow morning I'll give my testimony. Surely the members of the jury will understand and believe that it was an accident. Once they have heard my story it will be obvious to them that I loved my Harvey. Why else would a woman put up with so much crap for thirty-five years if not for love? Yes, I loved my Harvey. Soon I'll be going home.

NO STONE UNTURNED

The residents of Dudleyville were greatly saddened by the latest turn of events. Their leader, His Royal Highness The Dudley was said to be in poor health. It was even said that it was possible he was at death's door. With no direct heir to continue his reign there was a good possibility that the animal citizens of Dudleyville would again fall under the tyranny of human dictatorship once held by the dastardly race called Man.

King Dudley lay on his death bed. He was attended by his faithful human servants who loved him and supported his philosophy that dogs and, indeed, all animals were to be revered, loved and respected for their unfailing ability to offer unconditional love to all;

even to humans despite long held painful memories of their barbaric treatment toward them.

King Dudley was a dog and it was because of his untiring efforts to bring about reform and change that animals reigned over the human inhabitants of Dudleyville. At the age of ninety-six in human years King Dudley's memory was still intact. His brave, loving heart was strong but he knew it would soon be time to leave his body behind in order to ascend to the Rainbow Bridge. He must take steps to ensure that his animal subjects will not revert to slavery under the cruelty of human masters once he died and was no longer the Ruler of Dudleyville.

King Dudley, being descendant of the Jack Russell Terrier Tribe, had a small physique however throughout his years of reign in Dudleyville, Canada, he grew in wisdom and in stature. All in the international animal world looked up to him with adoration and respect; even the black bear and even the birds of all sizes from the beautiful black Raven down to the tiniest humble, hovering hummingbird.

Dudley's intelligence was of the highest order matched only by his unfailing ability to bring other animals together in order to plan and to implement ways and means to continue the stability and safety of life in Dudleyville. He ordered his human servants to send invitations to all committee chair animals including Mouse, leader of the Canadian Cat realm. He knew that Mouse could always be relied upon to share his quiet wisdom and sensible ideas. Aware that Mouse was almost as ancient as himself, he made sure that the roster of chair animals included some of the younger generation so, of course, the young, lovable and affectionate Mya was called to attend the meeting. And to be sure that the female animals were fairly represented the loyal, if somewhat outspoken Terrier, Mrs. Biggles would also be present.

Twelve animals in all would be called together. Because he did not feel capable of leaving his bed to journey into the conference room the meeting would take place in the King's bedroom. His humans provided cushions, blankets, food; all that was needed for his comfort and to ensure the ease of his invited guests. Dudley had trained his human servants well. His art of manipulation was so expert that the humans often thought that ideas and thoughts were their own. And, indeed, throughout their journey as servants to the king they had, indeed, learned to love, respect and adore him.

Dudley knew that his servants were not the only humans who loved their Masters; not the only ones who served with a willingness and devotion. Yes, he was aware that in Dudleyville there were many but he was also aware that there were many who, until they were either imprisoned or banished from the Dudleyville Realm, treated their animals like slaves with unrelenting cruelty.

Dudley's greatest fear was that upon his death these malicious humans would return to Dudleyville and free from jail the others of the Man variety. He prayed that the members of the Animal Council, once gathered together, would come up with a positive plan to keep the status quo; to keep the Dudleyville animals in power over the evil race of Man. He also hoped this conference would be helpful to animals throughout the entire planet of Earth. His greatest desire was to see the example he had set emulated throughout the world.

Dudley, because of his old age, had memory of how it used to be. He knew that dogs were often tied by rope and left without food or drink for hours alone to suffer in the hot summer sunshine and the harsh icy cold of winter. He knew that cats were often swung by their tails by some young members of the Man Race. He had heard many stories about Man who, with his guns and rifles, shot birds and animals, large and small, for entertainment. He knew even the fish in the lakes and seas were not safe from Man's greediness and hunger for power. He remembered that many dogs fell to their death from the backs of pick-up trucks driven with reckless speed along highways. He remembered that many enslaved by Masters who died or who simply no longer wanted the animals were executed in gas chambers. These were a miniscule few of the too many horrendous acts inflicted upon innocent animal victims throughout Canada and, indeed, throughout the entire world. If he allowed himself to dwell for too long on the atrocities Man heaped upon members of the animal world King Dudley would fall into a deep depression and this was something that, even on his deathbed, he wanted to avoid.

He needed to be at his best for this all important conference. He planned to share his knowledge of the great legend of the stone passed on to him by a wise, old owl that he had met in his childhood years. It was the wisdom of this owl that convinced Dudley in his earliest years that he could rid Dudleyville of the tyrants. And so he did. It was a tiring, lengthy and sometimes discouraging process but now at the age of 96 the King could rest easy knowing that all evil humans were either in prison or banned from the realm. Those humans who were capable of demonstrating reverence, love and respect toward the animal kingdom were permitted to remain in Dudleyville as personal servants. These servants were loved and cared for by their animals.

Dudleyville was a small kingdom in a large world filled with suffering and sorrow. The kingdom was surrounded on all sides by enemy states ruled by Man. Dudley knew he could not save the entire world but if, by sharing the knowledge of the great legend, he could save Dudleyville from extinction he would die a happy terrier. And there was always the hope that other animals throughout the world would learn from the example set by Dudleyville residents. There was always the hope that animals would stand up and refuse to be enslaved any longer.

King Dudley had little hope that Man would come to his senses and learn to live in love instead of hatred, greed and selfishness but he knew that even where there was the tiniest flicker of hope there was possibility, albeit remote, for change and reform throughout the world.

Invitations were sent out and the meeting was called to order. Dudley, from the comfort of his bed, chaired the meeting. The twelve committee representatives sat in a semicircle surrounding his bed. Present were Mouse, chair of the Cat Committee; Mya, chair of the Large Dog committee; Sara, chair of the Bird Committee. Mrs. Biggles was there representing the female animals. Bruce, chair of the Bear Committee and Edward, a large Mississaugi Rattle Snake who was chair of the Exotic Animal Committee also formed part of the semicircle around the King's bed. All of these animals were citizens in the Continent of North America.

In addition to these, present at the conference were representatives of the six other continents of the world. It took great ingenuity to bring these six international representatives to Canada but news of

Dudley's achievements had brought hope to even the most suffering of animals around the world.

From Asia came Tyrone, representing the Tigers who were severely endangered. From Africa came Charles, one of the Congo's Gorillas who were in dire need of help. South America's representative was an Andean Cat by the name of Andrew. On behalf of European animals the Brown Bear, Benedict, arrived from Italy and from Australia, Kenneth the Kangaroo represented all animals, large and small, who eked out an existence throughout the Australian continent. From Antarctica came Paul, the Penguin. It had been a very long and dangerous trip for him but he did arrive and was present at the Dudleyville Conference Concerning Freedom from Fear and Fatality at the Hands of Man.

King Dudley had selected these representatives with deliberate care knowing that each had earned the respect of all animals throughout their domain. By sharing the great legend with these world leaders he prayed that no stone would be left unturned and that peace would become an integral part of an animal's existence; that all animals could live free from fear of the relentless, murderous Man.

The hour had arrived. King Dudley, though physically weak, retained a strong, majestic rule over his own emotions and he felt a very strong spiritual connection to the Higher Power who had taught the truth of the legend to Wise Owl. Grateful that Owl had shared the pearls of wisdom with him, Dudley now prepared to share the truth of the legend with all present at the conference.

He began by welcoming everyone. With the exception of Sara, a tiny budgie who represented all birds of the world, he was physically the smallest animal in attendance but, make no mistake, he was the greatest in tolerance, love and understanding. They all looked to him for guidance.

Knowing this, King Dudley did not want to disappoint his animals. He prayed to his Higher Power for continued strength and wisdom. Then he told the story of the stone.

There is a stone, he said, that, if held by an animal in possession of a caring, kind heart, will spread goodness and kindness throughout the hearts of Man thereby making him open his eyes and his mind to a path whereupon he will be love. Not only will Man learn to love one another but he will also learn to love all animals of the earth, fish of the sea and birds of the air.

This stone is like no other on earth. Although I have not seen it myself I have been taught by Wise Owl that it is light green in colour. It is round with a

diameter of approximately two inches. It gleams in the
sunlight and it is one of a kind.

I am asking each of you to share this knowledge
with the animals, birds and fish throughout the earth.
Begin the search. Leave no stone unturned. We are all
endangered if left solely in the hands of Man. I beg of
you. Turn the world upside down if need be in order to
find this stone. It is green, the colour and texture of
love.

King Dudley blessed all in attendance. He even
thanked his human servants for a job well done. With a
cry from the depths of his soul he pleaded, let there be
love. The King died.

All committee members stood and together they
shouted, "The King is dead. Long live the King."

Soon after that time all animals returned to their
homes. They did share the truth of the legend of the

stone with all their peers. The search began and as of this writing the search continues. Animals throughout the world pray that the green stone of love will be held by a wise animal. They pray the day will come when humans throughout the world will finally stop the cruelty, the neglect, and the killing. They pray that all can live free from fear in peace and harmony.

It was not long after the death of King Dudley that Dudleyville ceased to exist. There was no heir to the throne. His humble human servants prayed that Man would come to his senses but before long Dudleyville was just another small part of a larger city in a greater country that, like the rest of the world, knew nothing of the legend of the stone. While animals throughout the earth continued their struggle for survival leaving no stone unturned in their search for the green stone of love, Man, with some exceptions, continued his selfish stride through life filled with undeserved pride; filled with greed and disregard for the innocent animals who, through no fault of their own, were victims of Man's arrogance, conceit and lack of good conscience.

King Dudley looked down upon the suffering animals. He stood upon the Rainbow Bridge and from that high vantage point he could look down upon the land. He could see the green stone of love. He hoped the day would soon come when an animal on earth would also see it and allow its power to flow through him. He prayed for the day when animals would rule the world and live with one another and, even with those humans willing to set aside their own hostilities and arrogance.

He had tried and he had met with success. His humble servants would love him forever. His loving reign would never be forgotten. God bless King Dudley. Long live the King.

THE BIG BOOK

Forty-seven year old Gwendolyn was lost for words. Her legs trembled as she stood before the pearly gates and listened to the judgment of St. Peter. Surely I must be hearing things, she thought. That's when she decided to try to argue her case.

"St. Peter," she pleaded, "my time on earth was very short but surely if you have everything about me recorded in that big book you must know my heart was in the right place."

Peter responded with unquestionable authority. "Gwendolyn, I've been watching you. There is no doubt we have a problem here. There is a distinct question mark behind your name."

"Oh, dear, won't you please let me in?"

"The gates are locked for you I'm afraid."

Distraught, Gwendolyn began to weep. "Is there no way I can change your mind?" she tearfully begged. "There is nothing I won't do. Please let me in?"

"Hmm," St. Peter considered while calmly caressing his white bearded chin. "Do you sincerely want to go to heaven?"

"Oh, yes, there is nothing I desire more than to go to meet my Master."

Peter pointed to a small plastic basket beside the heavenly gates then raised his eyes and spoke aloud to an invisible someone, "Socks, my Lord? Fill it with socks? Not rocks but socks?"

The loud voice boomed, "Are you questioning my authority?"

"Never, my Lord, never!" Peter answered. Bringing his gaze back to Gwendolyn he said, "You must take this basket with you and return to earth. I will give you ten days to fill this basket with socks."

"With socks?" What does the good Lord want with a basket full of socks?"

"Ours is not to question why," Peter answered. "Ours is but to......"

"I know, I know. I've already died, haven't I?" Gwendolyn argued. "I thought I had already made the greatest sacrifice. Now I am to go back home and collect socks?"

"Yes, exactly," St. Peter agreed. "I will give you ten days to complete this mission. You must acquire one sock from everyone you speak to on your return to earth.   Fill this basket with socks within ten days and you will be given permission to enter the pearly gates into heaven."

"Any kind of socks?" Gwendolyn asked. "Must they be woolen socks or cotton socks?"

"No, they can be made of any fabric known to man."

"Does it matter what colour they are?"

"No, no," St. Peter responded. "They can be any colour of the rainbow."

"How on earth am I supposed to convince people to give me a sock?" Gwendolyn asked. "I know God's ways are mysterious and not to be questioned but why on earth does God want a basket full of socks?"

Then looking at the yellow plastic basket she said, "At least, thank God, it is a very small basket."

She picked the basket up. She turned it over. "Hmm," she said, "made in China. Even in heaven everything is made in China?"

St. Peter laughed, "You are not in heaven yet, my child."

"And it has to be socks?" Gwendolyn persisted wondering how on earth she would persuade people to give her one of their socks. "Can it be a necktie instead or a glove? I believe it would be easier to convince someone to give up their underwear rather than a sock!"

Again St. Peter laughed, "I'm looking in the Big Book and there does seem to be some mention of past underwear removal. Could this be why the gates are locked for you today, my child?"

Embarrassed Gwendolyn blushed but simply said, "Why, I never!"

"The Book holds the truth. There is no denying truth if you want to pass through heaven's gate." St. Peter responded.

"Oh, dear, this isn't at all what I expected," Gwendolyn sighed.

"Off you go now. You can't continue to hold up the line like this. The people behind you are getting very impatient," Peter ordered. "Remember now, one sock from each person you speak to on earth."

"Oh, dear, I will need to be very selective in whom I choose to speak," Gwendolyn decided.

Looking again into the Big Book, Peter said, "Hmm, seems that is something else you should have thought about while living on earth. Oh, well, what's done is done. Off you go now. Come back in ten days and we will talk again."

"If I can fill the basket in less than ten days will I be allowed to gain entry? Will that be acceptable to our Lord?"

"Yes, my child. But that may be easier said than done. Now off you go and God be with you."

And just like that Gwendolyn looked around astonished to find herself standing on the Toronto street corner of Yonge and Eglinton just a few blocks from the apartment in which she had lived. Her first thought was to go home to her apartment, make a cup of tea and relax in her Lazyboy chair while she planned her sock hunting escapade. Will that door be locked to me too, she wondered realizing that it was in her favourite chair she was sitting when she suddenly arrived at the pearly gates. I had some pain in my chest, she remembered.

And now I am homeless in Toronto with no money. My only possession is this cheap yellow plastic basket and my only purpose in life is to collect a sock from every person to whom I speak. Such a stupid purpose, she thought as she tried to remember if she had ever been aware of any purpose at all during the forty-seven years she had lived on earth.

Suddenly it began to pour rain. The yellow plastic basket atop her head offered little protection. She ran for the nearest storefront doorway. Huddled in the corner of the entrance Gwendolyn peered through the window and realized that as luck would have it she was in the doorway of a shoe store. She stood there considering whether or not she should enter the store when a fellow came dashing in out of the rain. He shook his umbrella before closing it sending a wet spray into Gwendolyn's face.

"Watch what you're doing then!" she growled immediately regretting her words.   She knew that by speaking to this stranger she was obligated to somehow get him out of one of his socks.

"Sorry," the young man replied, "I didn't see you there."

Gwendolyn was simply dumbstruck, not knowing what to do or what to say to get this man to give up a sock.   I must think of something, she decided, or I will remain a homeless street person forever.

Then she remembered that she and the young man were standing in the doorway of a shoe store. Looking heavenward she wondered if St. Peter was offering her some sort of guidance.

"This is quite a downpour," the young man said. "I'm on my way to a job interview. I don't want to arrive there looking like a drowned rat."

"A job interview you say? And you are going to a job interview wearing those shoes?"

The young man looked down at his wet feet. "What's wrong with these shoes?"

"You're all dressed up in your blue suit and tie and you're wearing running shoes to an important job interview?"

"Oh," he replied, "I was hoping no one would notice that. They're good shoes. I paid over a hundred bucks for them."

Pleased with her own clever quick thinking Gwendolyn replied, "I don't care if you paid a thousand bucks for them they're still running shoes, are they not?"

"Yes, ma'am."

"Is it a job interview for a running courier?"

"No, ma'am."

"Well, son, I wonder why a bright boy like you wouldn't think to wear a decent pair of dress shoes to an important job interview?"

The young man looked sheepish, eyes downcast.

"What time is your job interview?"

Looking at his wristwatch he said, "I have a half hour to get there and it's just a block away. I allowed myself lots of time not wanting to be late."

"Well," Gwendolyn continued, "consider this your lucky day.   We happen to be standing in the doorway of a shoe store.   Had you noticed? "

"No, I hadn't actually."

"No arguments now," Gwendolyn prodded. "Let's get into this store and get you a new pair of shoes."

Smiling now, the young man agreed. "Good idea, thank you."

Inside the store now Gwendolyn tapped the young man on his arm and said, "If you really want to thank me.....

"Oh, I do. Of course I do."

"Well, then, since you really want to thank me, while you are buying your new pair of shoes you will also spring for a new pair of socks. Those you are wearing are soaking wet anyway. "

"Why do you want me to buy a new pair of socks?"

"So I can have your old ones; well, just one of your old ones actually."

"Why do you want my old sock?"

"Oh, Lord," Gwendolyn sighed. "Can't you just humour me?   Do I need to give you a reason for wanting your old sock?"

Laughing, the young man said, "I think that's the craziest thing I've ever heard but, no, if you want my old sock you've got it."

Once fitted with dry socks and shiny new shoes the young man was ready to confidently go to his job interview. Handing one of the old socks to Gwendolyn he said, "A deal's a deal. Here's your sock."

"Just put it into this little basket, will you, son?"

They left the store together. The clouds had disappeared and the sun shone once again. "Thanks for your good advice, ma'am. Nice meeting you!"

"Good luck on your interview, son"

Gwendolyn stared at the little yellow plastic basket in her hand. She looked at the small space the young man's sock filled and realized she had her work cut out for her. As small as this basket is I am going to need at least six or seven socks to fill it, she realized. She also realized she was getting hungry. "I thought dead people weren't supposed to feel hungry," she said aloud to herself.

"Excuse me?" The pretty young woman asked. "Were you talking to me?"

Gwendolyn took her time sizing up this young woman standing before her. Do I want to talk to her, she asked herself knowing that if she did she would need to acquire a sock from her. Gwendolyn looked down and smiled when she saw that the young lady was indeed wearing socks inside running shoes not so very different from the ones the young man had been wearing. Her decision made she spoke, "I was just saying that I was beginning to feel hungry."

The young woman looked at the plump middle-aged woman standing before her. She saw that her cotton dress was barely dry and wrinkled from the earlier downpour. She saw the small yellow plastic basket in her hand and wondered why the woman was carrying around an old damp sock. Recognizing

Gwendolyn as a street person she offered, "I'm just on my way to lunch. Would you like to join me?"

"Oh, that's very sweet of you, love. Thank you, yes, I would like that very much"

Extending her right hand the young woman introduced herself. "I'm Marilyn and there's a McDonald's just down the street."

Shifting the yellow plastic basket from her right to her left hand, Gwendolyn shook hands with the young woman. As they walked down Yonge Street she tried to imagine ways to encourage Marilyn to give up one of her socks. When they entered the restaurant together she still had no idea how she would achieve her goal.

"You pick a table and sit," Marilyn instructed. "I'll get the food and be right with you."

Gwendolyn sat down and watched as Marilyn walked toward the fast food counter. She noticed that the young woman had a slight limp and wondered if this was another guiding light from above.

Marilyn returned with two Big Mac's and two cups of coffee.

"Thank you," Gwendolyn said smiling into the friendly blue eyes of her new friend.

"Hope you don't think I'm rude but I noticed you are limping. Have your hurt your foot?

"Oh, it's nothing much," she replied. "These runners are just a little tight on me. Usually I wear a thinner sock but this morning in my rush to get out of the house I pulled on these wool socks that are making my feet very uncomfortable. I didn't realize I was limping to tell you the truth."

Raising her eyes heavenward Gwendolyn silently prayed thank you God for small mercies. Then with a big smile between bites of her Big Mac she said, "Well, for heaven's sakes girl, if the socks are causing your problem why don't you just take them off? You could wear those running shoes without socks. With the slacks you have on no one would even notice that you weren't wearing socks and your feet would feel much better."

"Now why didn't I think of that?" Marilyn laughed.

Gwendolyn laughed along with her and said, "I'm glad I am here to help you since you've been such a help to me buying my lunch and all but there is just one thing I hope you don't mind me asking."

"Sure, what is it?" Marilyn asked as she leaned over to unlace her shoes.

"Would you be kind enough to give me one of your socks?"

Oh, so she's looking for a pair of socks, Marilyn realized, but then she looked into Gwendolyn's smiling round face and knew she couldn't refuse the request. "Of course you can have my socks. I have plenty more at home."

"I just need one of your socks, love," Gwendolyn replied.

"Just one? Why do you want only one sock? What are you going to do with one sock?"

"It's a long story," Gwendolyn answered. "Do you have time to hear it?"

By this time Marilyn had removed her socks and was retying her shoes. Standing up she said, "Yes, this does feel much more comfortable. Thanks again,

Gwendolyn, but I'm afraid I haven't time to hear your story though something tells me it must be a good one." Glancing at her watch, then handing the socks over, she said, "Gotta run."

"No, no," Gwendolyn insisted, "just one sock please."

Taking one sock back and stuffing it into her rain jacket pocket the young woman smiled and said, "Okay, my friend. Take care of yourself now." She picked up the Big Mac containers and the empty coffee cups. Gwendolyn watched as she disposed of them in the trash can and then she was gone.

Gwendolyn remained sitting at the table. She carefully caressed and folded the pretty blue woolen sock and placed it in the plastic basket. The woolen sock took up much more space than the young man's thin cotton one. She realized that it would only take two or three more socks like this one to fill the basket.

With the yellow basket over her arm she left McDonalds and joined the rest of her world on the bustling city sidewalk. Since it was her old neighbourhood she knew it fairly well. With no destination in mind she allowed herself to be carried by the crowd. Travelling southbound she knew that eventually she would reach the busy intersection of Yonge and St. Clair. Remembering there was a park on St. Clair Avenue not far from Yonge Street she decided that would be a good safe place to spend her first night back in town.

Not wanting to make her task any more difficult than it needed to be she made a quick decision as she travelled not to talk to anyone unless that person was wearing socks, preferably large woolen ones. Carrying herself along she was beginning to enjoy herself. She felt quite proud of her prowess as she eyed the two socks in her little basket. Two socks and a lunch! A good start, she thought as she headed toward the park.

It was a beautiful summer's day as Gwendolyn turned off St. Clair onto the pathway that meandered through the small city park. She spotted a bench beneath one of the Maples and decided it would be a good place to spend the afternoon and maybe the night. She reached the bench and sat, yellow basket resting on her lap.

Suddenly out of nowhere a large dog came barreling down the pathway. Gwendolyn could see the loose leash fastened to his collar flying out behind him. "Oh dear," she worried, "what is in store for me this time?"

The large dog whizzed past her and then Gwendolyn saw the old lady running trying to catch the mischief-maker.   She must be at least eighty, Gwendolyn realized. Far too old to be running like this. As the woman approached the bench Gwen spontaneously shouted, "Be careful! You don't want to fall!"

The old lady stopped running. She wearily made her way to the bench and sat down beside Gwendolyn.   Gasping and trying desperately to catch her breath the old woman whispered, "My Bernard is getting away from me. Please, can you help me?"

"Don't worry; I'll get your dog back for you. Keep your eye on my basket, okay?" she asked.

"Yes, of course I will. Please hurry. My Bernard is all I have in this world since my Sidney died."

Gwendolyn took off running down the pathway after the big dog.   She ran for a good five minutes before she finally spotted him, leg up against the trunk of a big Maple.   "Good boy," she said. "Stay, good boy."

And stay he did. Gwendolyn took a firm grasp on the end of the leash and walked him back to the old lady sitting on the bench.

"Oh, Bernard," the old woman reprimanded, "you are such a bad boy running off like that." Turning to face Gwendolyn sitting next to her she said, "I am ever so grateful.   If I'd carried on running like that I'm sure I would have had a heart attack like my poor, dear Sidney did just last year."

"Oh, you don't want to have a heart attack," Gwendolyn warned. "Lord knows I did and now I am on a sock hunt."

"What?" the old lady asked.

"Oh, nothing, nothing at all. I was just making a bad joke."

"How can I repay you for your thoughtfulness?" the old lady asked.

Gwendolyn glanced down at the old lady's feet. She was wearing black panty-hose inside a pair of sturdy black walking shoes. No help for me at all, Gwendolyn realized. "I am glad I was able to help you, Missus. If you had a sock I'd take it but you don't and there is nothing else I need."

"A sock?" The old lady laughed. "What on earth are you talking about?" Holding Bernard's leash in her left hand she rested her cloth handbag on her lap as she reached her right hand up to her ear to adjust her hearing aid. "There that's better," she said. "Now tell me again. My hearing isn't the best and I thought I heard you say you wanted a sock."

"That's exactly right. See, I have two socks already. My goal is to fill this tiny plastic basket with socks. Nothing else is important to me anymore I'm afraid."

The old lady was astonished. "I don't understand but if you really want socks I have some socks here in my knitting bag. I've finished knitting one pair. No idea who they are for. I always knitted Sidney's socks and now I have no one to knit for anymore. Still I knit. What's an old lady to do?"

"You have socks in that bag?"

"Yes, yes, I have three socks and another half-way made."

"I can't believe my good luck!" Gwendolyn shouted. "Please, will you give me one of those socks?"

"Well, seems very strange to me but if you are sure that's what you want then of course you can have one of my socks. If it wasn't for your help I wouldn't have my precious Bernard. Giving you a sock is the least I can do for you. Which one do you want?" she asked displaying three large men's socks.

"You keep the pair of blue ones. I'm sure you will find someone who can wear them. I will accept the red one and I am very grateful."

The old lady handed the large red sock to Gwendolyn. "Thank you again," she said then turning to her dog the old lady stood up, tugged a little on the leash and said, "Bernard, no running! Do you understand? No running!"

Gwendolyn watched as the little old lady slowly walked away from her with Bernard obediently by her side. She smiled as she carefully folded the sock and placed it into her basket. It was a large sock and she was thrilled to realize that if she could get just one more large sock like this her basket would be filled.

Gwendolyn placed the little basket on the seat close to the back of the bench. Then curling her body around the basket she tried to make herself comfortable enough to get some sleep. She knew she must have dozed for a while because when she again opened her eyes she saw stars shining brightly in the night sky. Reaching for her basket she sat up on the bench and wondered what her next move should be.

She felt stiff from sleeping on the hard wooden bench. What I need is a good walk, she decided. Carrying the basket in her hand she followed the pathway out of the park and began walking west along

St. Clair Avenue toward Yonge Street. The main thoroughfare was filled with people, young and old. They seemed a cheerful bunch and Gwendolyn remembered when she was part of the Saturday night crowd out on a date on her way to a good restaurant or theatre. Those days are gone for me, she thought. Now I am just a shadow of myself; a silly woman in search of socks. If someone had told me I would be spending my time on such a useless errand I would have had a good laugh. I've never been a religious woman but I always thought that when I died I'd go to heaven and here I am, walking along Yonge Street on a Saturday night. I'm not looking for a good time. I'm just looking for socks. Crazy, she thought and suddenly she was laughing out loud at the ridiculous situation she was in.

"Having a good time, sweetheart?" he asked. "I love your laugh but what are you laughing at?"

This time when Gwendolyn turned toward the masculine voice she looked into the eyes of an elderly man.   She could see he was obviously drunk.   He stood on the sidewalk in front of her weaving back and forth. Then she noticed the brown paper bag in his hand but looking down she noticed something far more important. The old guy was wearing dirty brown socks beneath tattered old shoes.

The socks are pretty thin, she realized, but they are socks and I don't want to miss any opportunity.

"Having a good time, sweetheart?" the old man asked again.   "Do you want a little drinkie?"

Gwendolyn decided to speak.   "Just a little sip," she answered wondering if these tactics were the correct ones that would lead to achievement of her goal.

"Come on into the alley with me, baby.   I'll share my bottle with you."

Gwendolyn hesitated then thought what am I worried about? He can't kill me if I'm already dead. "I'll come into the alley with you on one condition," she stated.

"One condition? What condition you talking about? I'm not into making deals, you know. I just want to share a little drinkie-poo with you."

"It will cost you."

"Cost me? Are you a pro? Lordy, I never would have taken you for a pro, little lady. Aren't you too old for that kind of monkey business?"

Feeling insulted Gwendolyn replied, "Why, the nerve! I don't know which is the bigger insult; calling me a pro or telling me I'm too old to be one."

"Aah, I'm sorry lady. I didn't mean no insult, honest."

"Well, okay, but here's my condition. I will come into the alley and share a drink with you but in return I want you to give me a sock."

"You want me to sock you?" he asked in amazement. "Hey lady, I'm not into no violent stuff. I'm just a friendly fella looking for some company for a little while."

Gwendolyn could not contain her laughter. "You foolish man," she said. "I don't want you to sock me. I want you to give me one of your socks."

"You want one of my socks? Hey lady, I must be drunker than I thought. You want one of my stinky old socks?"

"Yep."

"Okay, lady. I never heard of anything more stupid but if you want it, you got it. Let's go," he said putting his arm around her shoulders.

Gwendolyn held on tightly to her little basket. "I'm dead," she reminded herself. "What on earth is there to fear?"

She spent an hour with the old man. She learned that his name was Benjamin and that he had been surviving on the lonely streets for nearly two years since his wife and grandchildren burned in the fire. "It was my fault," he told Gwendolyn. "My wife told me more than a couple of times to fix the wire on that heater but I was too damn lazy. It was all my fault."

"And you've been living on the streets since then? "Gwendolyn asked.

"Sure," he replied, "if you can call it living. I just go from day to day. I don't care about tomorrow."

"You're not so old that you can't still build a future for yourself," Gwendolyn told him sternly. "I want you to come with me to the Salvation Army Hostel where you can get yourself cleaned up and start over again."

"You think there's hope for me, lady?"

"There is hope for us all," she responded. "I'll walk there with you but you've got to do something for me first."

"What's that?" he asked.

"Take off your shoe and give me one of your socks."

And he did just that. Gwendolyn folded the dirty brown sock and added it to her pile. Just one more, she thought. One more and I can get through the gates. She left Benjamin at the hostel on Yonge Street.

It was growing late in the evening and she wondered where on earth she would spend the night.

She kept walking south on Yonge Street. She had walked a long way and was approaching Dundas Street. Across the road she saw the huge Eaton Centre and wondered if she would find a resting place there.

She crossed the street at the lights. People milled all around her, some staring at the strange woman in the thin cotton housedress carrying the little plastic basket almost filled with old socks but most people, used to strange city sights, ignored her as she passed them on her way through the giant mall.

Midway through the mall she stopped by the big water fountain. Taking a seat on one of the cement benches she looked up at the big birds hanging from the cathedral ceiling. Free as a bird, she thought. I used to feel free as a bird. Now I just feel plain tired. She knew security officers would not allow her to spend the night on a bench inside the mall. She knew she had to keep moving along.

She stood up and continued her walk toward the mall's exit. Out on the street once again she heard beautiful music. Walking toward the harmonious sounds she came upon a small group of musicians wearing Salvation Army uniforms. Beside them on the sidewalk was a table supporting huge pots of soup and a big coffeemaker. On the other side of the little band was another table containing a variety of items. There were jackets and sweaters and shoes and, God bless us all she thought, there were socks.

Approaching the table she stared at the socks knowing she had no money to buy them. Soon a young woman wearing one of those uniforms stood on the other side of the table across from her. "Do you see something you like?" the woman enquired.

"Is it possible I can take a sock?"

"You don't need to limit yourself to one sock, dear lady. Take a pair of socks and help yourself to a dress. I am sure we will have something here to fit you."

"Thank you for your kindness but I have need of one sock only. May I take one?"

The city street worker was used to strange people and Gwendolyn was just one more. "Of course, just help yourself."

Gwendolyn folded the large grey sock onto the top of the basket. The basket was full.

Then magically she was standing once more before St. Peter. He looked into the Big Book. The question mark was gone. "Well done, my child," he said. "You have filled the basket and in doing so you have helped others along their way. You gave much more than you received. This was your lesson to learn. Welcome home, my child."

The pearly gates swung open. Gwendolyn handed her basket to St. Peter then turned as she walked through, "It only took me a day but it was a very long day. Am I too late for supper?"

THE SILENT STAR

I must have had a father but to this day no one has introduced me to the man and he has made no attempt to contact me. Thirty-five years ago my mother, Fiona, lay weak in her hospital bed. I was later told that just moments before she died she held me in her arms and named me Andrew Joseph McPhail.

I don't clearly remember much soon after that. I lived in an orphanage throughout my earliest years. Once I was old enough I remember travelling in a group with all the other kids on our way to school. We formed a line and in pairs we marched along the big city sidewalks. We were led by a Sister at the front of the line and there was another who herded us, like little lost lambs, at the back of the line.

The first real home I remember outside of the orphanage was with the Farley family. I was six years old when I came to live with them. I spent three years in their happy, noisy, crowded Christian home.

I think it's because they were such a rowdy bunch in their daily living that I often felt lost in the shuffle and learned to keep to myself. Mrs. Farley would often ask me, "What's the problem, Andy? Why are you so quiet?"

I never seemed able to come up with a satisfactory answer to her question until during a church service one Sunday we sang a hymn. The lyrics went something like, *"For the everlasting right the silent stars are strong; all wrong shall stand revealed and every hurt be healed."*

To my nine year old ears those were pungent words. That morning I decided that come what may I would be a Silent Star. To her credit Mrs. Farley did her best to dissuade me from hiding in the protective silence and I did appreciate her efforts. I knew she cared about me but what neither of us understood was that I did not. Looking back on those days I realize that I wasn't seeing clearly. I went through life peering through a raster and trying to read between the lines.

I attended church every Sunday morning with the Farley family and it was during that time I first learned about the other Joseph; the one that is written about in the Bible. Every week I would sit scrunched in the middle of the third row with William Farley and the Farleys' son, Gordon, on my right; Mrs. Farley and their two daughters lined up on my left.

Because we were in church the Farleys were quiet for a change. The particular Sunday morning that seems to stand out in my memory now is when the Reverend Father MacFarlane was preaching as he always did. He was telling us all about Joseph's enslavement, imprisonment and his rise to the elevated status of Chief over Egypt. I identified strongly with Joseph. Had my real mom known the story of Joseph? I wondered if that was why I carried his name.

Soon the priest was summing up his sermon. "Just like Joseph," he was saying, "with faith and discipline in truth, we can rise up from the depths of despair and still overcome the burdens we carry."

I was glad the priest was finishing up. I was hungry. Soon we would all be on our way home to enjoy the delicious stew that Mrs. Farley had prepared the night before. She had seasoned it with coriander and it smelled delicious. I had wanted to eat some before I headed off to bed that night but she was adamant. "Andy McPhail," she said, "I know you want to eat this stew now but the closest you are going to come to that is in your dreams. Off to bed with you now! You'll have the stew for lunch like the rest of us tomorrow after church."

Well, I didn't dream of the stew that night but I was dreaming about it now as Father MacFarlane was finally coming to the end of his sermon. At the end of the service we all left the church. I piled into the back seat of the car with the Farley girls, Catherine and Mary. I would have preferred to sit in the front seat between the parents but Gordon always sat up there. He was the eldest boy and the biggest. Mr. Farley always drove. His name was William but everyone called him Willy. We were pulling out of the church parking lot. Fiona Farley never failed to say to her husband, "Don't drive too fast, Willy." This morning was no exception.

So I sat in the back seat as usual. Catherine and Mary were jabbering away about some female stuff that held no interest for me. I was hungry and my thoughts were centred on Mrs. Farley's tasty stew.

Then it happened. My world was black.

The next thing I remember I woke up in a hospital bed. When I opened my eyes I could see that Father MacFarlane was there sitting in a chair next to me. "I'm sorry, my boy. Poor wee lad all alone in this world again."

It hurt my face when I tried to talk but I had to know. "Father, what do you mean alone in this world again? What's happened Father?"

Just then the doctor came into the room. I saw the shake of the doctor's head and the sadness in Father MacFarlane's eyes. I didn't cry when he told me what had happened. I was frozen inside. I huddled deeper within and found the quiet spaces that lurked around outside my lonesome heart. I refused to let the pain

177

come into my heart. I was The Silent Star. My ears burned when they received the words, "There was an accident, Andrew. Willy and Fiona are both in Heaven now, son, and they've taken young Gordon along with them."

Words failed me but the kindly priest must have been able to read my thoughts. He answered my question without me having to ask. "Catherine and Mary are here in the hospital. They will be okay, God willing, and so will you, son. So will you."

I don't know if I was okay or not but in time I was released from the hospital and placed in another foster home. I was nine years old, soon to be ten. Catherine and Mary were not there to help me celebrate my birthday when it finally rolled around. To this day I don't know where the girls are. I hope they are okay but it isn't something I ever asked about or talked about. I knew how to keep my thoughts to myself.

I was the only child in this new foster home. I don't know who made the decision to put me into the house with Ike and his wife, Marta. I don't know why this happened to me but it did. I lived with the old couple for five years until I was fourteen years old. That is when I was finally able to take things into my own hands and do something about what was going on in that godforsaken place.

Marta was a very wise woman; an old crone; a spiritual woman who inspired me to believe that there was purpose in all things. I guess she was kind of like a grandma to me because she was a lot older than the mothers of the other kids who attended my school.

I couldn't tell her what Ike was doing. How could I? Ike made it clear to me that if I opened my mouth to anyone about those Saturday afternoons in the cellar he would take the axe down off the basement wall and chop my legs off. "I'll dwarf ya, you little bugger!" He'd threaten, "Not one word outa you, boy, if you don't wanna feel the bite of the axe."

I remained The Silent Star.

Marta faithfully took me to church on Sunday mornings. Like all good Catholic boys I went to confession but I never let Father MacFarlane know what was going on at home.

Father MacFarlane was a fan of Bob Dylan's music and he would sometimes quote from his song, *"Commit to act now about the hate that has grown. Let tolerance abide; and respect here be shown."* Deep inside of me I could feel the hate but I had little understanding of the words, tolerance and respect. I would listen to his sermons and try to make some connection between what he was saying and what Ike was doing to me.

When Marta attended her women's meetings at church on Saturday afternoons Ike would drag me down into the cellar. After a while it became routine. He didn't even need to threaten me. He would just point to the axe hanging on the wall and drive his piercing eyes into mine. I knew what I was supposed to do and I did it. And when I knelt on that cold hard cement cellar floor in front of him I felt nothing. I said nothing. I was nothing.

I was merely the observer; The Silent Star looking down on a horror that I refused to allow myself to feel.

When I was fourteen I sat in the pew next to Marta.

The day before down in the dark cellar Ike's routine changed. "You're growin' up, boy. Take 'em down. Let's see what you got!" he spat.

I remember I stood there like a statue staring at the axe while Ike knelt on that cold hard cellar floor in front of me. Still I felt nothing. I was nothing.

The next day Marta took me to church with her as usual. Like I said I was fourteen and I sat in the pew next to Marta. Listening to Father MacFarlane, I thought he must really like the music of Bob Dylan more than I realized because in his sermon he was quoting again from one of his songs. *"So we'd better start swimming or we'll sink like a stone for the times they are a-changing."*

I held onto those words and that night before going to bed I took the Bible that Marta had given me out of the bedside drawer. I closed my eyes, opened the book and placed my pointed finger onto the page. In the silence I sought guidance. "Help me, God," I prayed.

I opened my eyes and looked down. The book was opened in Genesis, Chapter 40. I started to read. I learned that my namesake, Joseph, had correctly interpreted the dreams of the wine steward and the baker. In return the wine steward promised to help Joseph; to plead for his release from prison before the king. But that wasn't what happened. I read, *"The king restored the wine steward to his former position but he executed the chief baker. It all happened just as Joseph had said. But the wine steward never gave Joseph another thought - he forgot all about him."*

I thought about Joseph all alone in that prison. He was forgotten just like me. I focused hard on the words that I'd read and before I went to sleep that night I had begun to formulate my plan of action. The king executed the chief baker. I knew what I had to do. The Silent Star would strike.

The following Saturday afternoon Marta left the house as usual to attend her church women's meeting. As usual I descended the stairs with Ike right behind me hurrying me along. When we reached the bottom of the stairs I watched as Ike's eyes turned and landed on the axe hanging on the cement block wall.

The Silent Star didn't waste a second. I turned, reached up and grabbed the axe from the wall. I remember screaming, "Help me, God!"

I was fourteen years old and a lot shorter than Ike. I swung the axe. I lopped off his legs. I dwarfed him. His bloody legs collapsed and his body splotched onto the cellar floor. Blood spattered everywhere. It was all over my hands, my body, and my face. It felt sticky and warm at first, almost hot and wet, but then it became as hard and cold as my heart. Just like the king dealt with the chief baker, I executed Ike.

Had he given me a fair chance? No! Even as I stood there alone, a self-convicted murderer, I drew strength from the words of a hymn we sometimes sang in church, *"Proclaim the day is near, the day in whose clear-shining light all wrong shall stand revealed."* It was time for the world to know the truth about Ike Campbell.

I felt a little sorry for Marta. She was the one who found us in the cellar when she came home from the meeting. It wasn't her fault. She didn't know and I didn't tell her.

I vaguely remember the trial. I set The Silent Star aside and basically I spilled my guts. I told the truth; everything that had been done to me by Ike. I don't know if anyone believed me or not.

Because I was just fourteen they didn't send me to the federal prison at that time. Instead they sent me to a boys' reformatory. They kept me there until I was twenty-one. At that time I stood before a Judge again. I didn't say much but somehow the Judge was convinced that I was reformed and I was free at last.

I didn't know what to do with the freedom. A social worker named Tom found me a job in a local brewery. I spent the next couple of years making beer. By this time if anyone ever asked me my name I'd just nod and quietly say, "Call me The Silent Star." Co-workers caught on fast and left me alone. The boss didn't bother me either because I minded my own business. I kept my nose to the grindstone and did a good job.

I no longer attended church. But I often thought about Father MacFarlane and his sermons. During the time I worked in the brewery I thought about the wine steward who had been released from prison and restored to his former position just as Joseph had correctly interpreted his dream and predicted. I still identified with Joseph but I knew I wasn't going to be restored to any former position because I didn't have one. I didn't want to remember any former anything so I didn't but, just like Joseph of the Bible, I would go to sleep and have vivid dreams.

Often I would have dreams that plagued my waking hours. The dreams were not nightmarish. They were simply elusive. Always in my dreams I would be in a beautiful rose garden where it was calm, peaceful and serene.

My dreams made no sense to me. They held no relevance to my reality. As foolish as it sounded even to me I wished Joseph would come into my dreams and interpret them for me. But, of course he didn't. I did love the rose garden I often dreamed of though and I got into the habit of keeping a red rose in a bud vase on top of the dresser in my room. I didn't know why the rose was so important to me. I just knew that it was.

I was twenty-three years old when I met Eddie Morrison. He was hired on at the brewery and though I never went out of my way to talk to him he seemed to want to hang around with me. He'd talk a blue streak. I'd say as little as possible. We worked side by side at the brewery and after a couple months I agreed to go to a bar with him after work to meet a couple of his mates and have a drink or two.

I was nobody going nowhere. So when one night in the bar Eddie and his pals planned the break-in I just sat there saying nothing. I let them con me into driving the get-away car. Eddie led his buddies into the dark, empty house. It was obvious to me sitting in the car outside that there was nobody home. When the alarm sounded the three guys came tearing out of the house, into the car. "Move it, Andy! Get us out of here!" they all screamed.

My foot hit the accelerator. We were flying. It wasn't long before the sirens were chasing us.

We all could have been killed but nobody died. I didn't die. I thought maybe it's hard to die when you are already dead inside. Maybe we are not allowed to die until we know we have lived.

This time the Judge sent me to federal prison for two years. While I was in jail I was visited by the prison pastor. He gave me a Bible. For a long time I didn't even look at the book. I just stuck it away in a drawer and forgot about it.

But when I'd been incarcerated for a few months the dream returned. Each night, again, I would be in the rose garden. I was waiting. But the dream never revealed what I was waiting for."

I didn't understand the connection but the dreams somehow encouraged me to reach for that Bible. I was drawn to Genesis, chapter forty. I read that story over and over again while I was in prison. I totally identified with Joseph and his ability to interpret dreams; his rise to Chieftain over Egypt.

I knew there was a transcendent correlation between Joseph's experience and my own future. I knew my visits to the rose garden in my dreams were key to understanding myself but that's as far as I was able to get in my own interpretation of things.

I kept to myself in prison, stayed out of trouble and the two years passed.

Once out of jail again I bounced from one job to another. It seemed that, for me, nothing had changed and, as usual, I was nobody going nowhere. When I got my pay cheque I would buy a bottle, hole up in my room and stay there until the bottle was empty.

There were times when I would think about my real mother and wonder what she had been like. That would lead me to wonder who my father was. Then I would think about the Farleys; Marta the old crone. When thoughts turned to Old Ike I would tear out of my room and not return until I'd bought another bottle.

By the time I was twenty-six I was drinking so much I couldn't wake up to get to a job on a Monday morning. Though I've been rambling on for a while you could say that this is when my story really starts.

I was a bum.

I lost my job and with no income I soon lost the roof over my head. I was alone; a homeless drunk pan-handling on the streets of Toronto. I slept on the warm grids allowing the heat from the subway to warm my weary bones. Sometimes I slept in the doorways of the stores on Yonge Street until the cops came and made me get up. "Move along," they would order. And I would move along until I could find a place where I could safely sit. I'd upturn my old cap and hold it in my hand begging for enough change to buy myself a bottle of cheap wine.

And that is exactly what I was doing when I met Rose.

It was a gray Monday morning but when I raised my eyes to look into hers I felt as though I were bathing in the hot sun's rays. She wasn't like most people who either blindly walked past me or simply flipped a dime or a quarter into my hat. No, when I looked up into her warm eyes she looked down into mine.

At once I was aware of myself and how I must appear to her; a ragged, drunken bum going nowhere but downhill into oblivion.

She took her hand out of her coat pocket and reached down. I thought she was going to slip me a coin but instead she stood there with her right hand outstretched in front of me. "Hello," she said, "my name is Rose."

I felt the shivers race through my body. I felt the love of God shining His face upon me. I knew she was my dream and my dream of the rose was coming true. She was my Rose. I felt I was in timelessness. Thoughts, feelings, emotions were working their way through me yet time stood still. I was aware and insightful. I thought of Joseph and somehow I believed he was interpreting my dream. I was alone in the rose garden and Rose would be my salvation.

And she was. That day and for several days after that Rose would stop and visit with me in my homeless storefront abode. It was her good advice that led me to the agency which hired me to hand out pamphlets on the street. It was Rose's loving hand that led me to my first AA meeting. And it was Rose who took me shopping in the St. Vincent de Paul store where I was finally able to shed the old torn jeans and dirty shirt that hung like a sign on my back which read, *"Nothing going nowhere."*

I had been handing out pamphlets on the street for several weeks but my life was such a haze that it was a while before I finally sat down with Rose and read one of those pamphlets. I was taken aback when I first became aware that the pamphlet contained an invitation to an outdoor church. And on the front cover of the pamphlet was a quotation from the Bible. The quotation was from Genesis, Chapter forty and it read,

"It is God who gives the ability to interpret dreams."

Below the quotation were the words, *"Just like Joseph you can come from the depths of despair and still overcome the burden you carry as long as you have faith and discipline in truth."*

I read the words and I knew this was no coincidence. This was the hand of God reaching out to me through the loving hand of Rose. I was in despair. I had no hope of a future. My life was meaningless. But then I met Rose and through her I came to know God. I came to know that through God all things are possible. If God brings us to it, whatever the situation may be, God will bring us through it and He will bring us through it victorious.

Rose led me to someone who helped me through the bitter sweetness of spiritual psychotherapy. I began to understand that I was not just a nobody. Terrible things had been done to me and I have done terrible things but I am somebody. In God's eyes I am. I count for something.

For many years I was The Silent Star. But now I shout it from the rooftops. Today I stand here in this sacred shelter, in this pulpit. My lovely wife, Rose, sits here beside me. Today I minister to you, my friends. You may be homeless in the eyes of the world. You may feel lonely and alone. Circumstances have shaped you and made you into Silent Stars but with God's help you will find your voice as I, thanks to Rose, have done. And, when you do, all that you have experienced will be shared. Through this sharing you will help others to find a home; their rightful place on God's good earth.

I've been rambling on here for a long time. If you want to call what I've been doing preaching, then I believe this sermon has been longer than any I ever heard from Father MacFarlane but I thank you good people for listening. I have shared my story with you. I hope my story finds a home in your heart. If you have faith, even if that faith is as small as a mustard seed, know that God is listening. He knows your pain.

Just as the king restored the wine steward to his former position, God will restore you to your former self and make you whole again. He, who makes the lame to walk; the sick to heal, hears your every prayer. You may be homeless in the eyes of the world but if you will open the door when God knocks you will find you are never alone again. Won't you stand and sing with me? *"Amazing grace, how sweet the sound to save a wretch like me. I once was lost but now I'm found; was blind but now I see."*

JIE KE'S TEA HOUSE

His father calls him plain stubborn. His mother can't seem to stop crying. She is on the verge of nervous collapse. His grandfather begs him to sit with him; to be quiet and listen to his stories of bygone days when the rumble of approaching horses' hooves shaking the earth meant certain death for those who dared to remain in Canada. But Jie Ke was determined. He would not be moved.

He accepted that he was rarely, if ever, understood by his family. He was the first in his family to be born in Canada. He was born July 10, 1922; the Year of the Horse.

At the time of Jie Ke's birth his father, An de lu, was already thirty years old and a carpenter by trade. It was his father who named the first born Jie

Ke. To celebrate his son's entry into the world he arranged delivery from Cameroon in Central Africa of a large block of Zebrano wood. This striking and very expensive wood was a pale golden yellow with here and there streaks of dark brown to black. From this Zebrano An de lu carved, in the most intricate detail, a rocking horse.

From the earliest age Jie Ke excelled in the handling and saving of money. He had a dream and unlike most who were born in the Year of the Horse he never lost sight of his goal. He left his father's house at an early age and remained restless, hopping from one meaningless short-lived job to another, but always he was focused on the dream of establishing his own business.

His mother, Ma Sha, was never happy with his plan. It wasn't that she objected to him having a business of his own; she was alarmed because the business her son wanted to establish was a tavern. True to her Buddhist religion which totally rejected the consumption of alcohol she was humiliated and embarrassed by Jie Ke's desire to serve sinful drinks to the public. She prayed for the increase of her son's spiritual knowledge. She begged her husband to convince their son to change his plans.

An de lu did his best to please his wife. "You are not a horse," he exclaimed. "You are a mule; stubborn and unrelenting!" But Jie Ke turned a deaf ear to his father's protestations.

Most Chinese immigrants in the 1950's were the wives and children of men already settled in Canada. This wasn't the case in Jie Ke's family. Ma Sha came to join her husband in Canada in 1921. Jie Ke had the good fortune to be born a Canadian citizen the following year.

His parents' objections to his business plan angered Jie Ke. "I am not Chinese," he insisted. "I am Canadian. I am not a Buddhist! And I am not Jie Ke. My name is Jack. Make no mistake, I will open my business. I'm going to call it Jack's Tavern. No one; not you and definitely not grandfather will get in the way to stop me. I will achieve my goal whether you like it or not!"

"Think of this, my son," his father said. "If you had not been born Canadian in 1922 the following year this country would not have allowed you to enter. Surely you have felt the discrimination, son. If you open this tavern you will be discriminated against. Don't you know that Chinese people observe Canada Day as Humiliation Day? On July 1, 1923 Chinese immigration was banned. Don't you realize what we have suffered? Think of all that your mother has had to endure.

How can you add to her sense of humiliation by opening a tavern? Have you no respect for your parents?"

Jie Ke was unaware that his grandfather, Yue se tu, had shared many stories of intolerance and harassment with his son. Wishing to look to a brighter future, An de lu did not, in turn, pass these stories along.

Now, faced with his son's stubborn refusal to listen, An de lu wondered if this had been a big mistake. If he had made his son more aware of the suffering of his ancestors he would become more tolerant and compassionate toward his parents. An de lu decided that where he had failed to tame his wild son, the boy's grandfather, Yue se tu, would succeed.

With reluctance Jack agreed to meet with his grandfather on the condition that his parents would not be present. He neither wanted more criticism from his father nor did he desire to witness more of his mother's tears.

Together the two men sat at the kitchen table. Yue se tu smiled at his grandson and said, "You were born in 1922. I was born in 1862. This means that I am sixty years wiser than you."

"Ha! Sixty years wiser or simply sixty years older? Why do you assume I possess less wisdom than you, Grandfather?"

"Jie Ke, you are young and you are stupid. You think you are smart to open a tavern? This action is not smart. You are a smart ass; a donkey. Yet we know you were born in the Year of the Horse. This means that somewhere hiding very deep within you there is the ability to be intelligent. It is this intelligence I wish to reason with; not the smart-ass know-it-all who refuses to consider the wisdom of his elders."

"Grandad, Jack's Tavern can be a place where people come together to socialize; to relax after a hard day of working. What can be wrong with this?"

"Jie Ke, if you had opened a tavern in Vancouver's Chinatown in 1907 you would have had a mob of thousands crashing and breaking your windows. In those days white Canadians were free to demonstrate their hatred of Chinese people. There was no law; no consequences for their cruel actions."

"I don't live in the past, Grandad. This is 1952. I am a thirty year old Canadian. No one is going to throw rocks through the window of my tavern.

"Jie Ke, this intolerance existed not only in Vancouver. Did you know that in 1919, just three years before you were born, hundreds of soldiers and civilians rampaged through downtown Halifax? They swept into Chinese-run cafes to break furniture, steal goods and loot cash registers."

"Grandfather, what does any of that have to do with me? I am not an immigrant. I am born in this country. No one is going to sweep into my tavern to break furniture and steal from me."

"Grandson, do you understand what your opening of a tavern would do to your mother?"

Jack had no response to offer. He sat on a chair across from Yue se tu who now sat with hands quietly folded in a prayerful posture. He rose to leave saying, "I will consider all you have told me, Grandfather."

"I can ask no more than that of you, grandson."

That evening Jack sat alone in his room. He thought of his grandfather who, in his wisdom, never once told Jack he could not open a tavern but simply asked him to consider what such a decision would do to his mother.

In spite of his mother's desire that he be awakened in faith, Jack was not a religious man. In spite of his father's benevolent example, Jack was not compassionate nor was he wise in spite of his insistence on telling his Grandfather that he was. Jack realized that his family members were right. He was meant to be a horse but he was living life as a jack-ass. He realized that by creating unhappiness in the lives of his parents he would never find happiness for himself.

The following morning Jack arose with a sense of purpose. He smiled at his father and hugged his mother. "I want to talk to you both about Jack's Tavern," he calmly stated.

"Son, please," his mother begged, "I can talk no further about a tavern."

"I had hoped your meeting with your grandfather would wake you up but I see you are still asleep," his father said.

"Hear me out, Mom and Dad. I have a new name for my business. Do you want to know what it is?"

"I'm not sure," Ma Sha replied.

"I want to know," his father stated.

"*Jack's Tavern* will now be called *Jie Ke's Tea House*. My plan remains exactly the same. The only change will be what I serve in the glasses. My beautiful Zebrano wood rocking horse will have this name painted on its side. With pride it will sit in the storefront window. Do you approve of my decision?"

His father placed his arm around his wife's shoulders. Ma Sha was overjoyed upon hearing her son's decision. "My son," she said, "If a man lives a pure life nothing can destroy him. You have become a lamp unto yourself."

THE SECOND SELF

(This is a story of extreme child abuse.)

It's not a simple matter to tell you who I am or why Steven created me. This is not an easy story to tell. I'm convinced I may disappear with the rush of water down the drain if only I can find a way to block the filthy language Steven has been forced to wade through since his mother died seven years ago. I can tell you he was barely out of babyhood, only three years old, when he was clad in his first pair of lederhosen and taught to worship at the feet of his grandfather, Heinrich Drescher who is the sick source of the venomous verbal diarrhea that permeates Steven's world.

I am Steven's second self. I am his sustenance. My name is Steve.

Steven lives in a room in the basement of an upscale suburban bungalow. This is a house with superb organized curb appeal. The basement windows hide behind deep green sprawling Junipers. No one would ever suspect that this neat, pristine, house is one of quiet horror. No one knows that a ten year old boy struggles to exist within its walls.

Upon his mother's death, being her only child, Steven was brought to this house of hate by a young, novice social worker over-burdened by a heavy case load that would have proven too much to handle even for someone with years of child welfare experience.

His mother, Susan, never had a husband. Her mother died when she was six and from then on she was raised by her father, Heinrich, whose verbal and emotional abuse was enough to cause her to run away from home at the age of fifteen. Desperate for love and affection, she had a series of boyfriends. When she discovered she was pregnant she did not know which boy was the father of her baby. That was of small importance to her. What mattered was that she was happy to know that finally she would have someone to love.

Susan did her best to provide a good, safe life for Steven. Though she experienced financial struggle on welfare she always put her child's needs first and was a good mother to her son. It was Steven's misfortune that his loving mom became a victim of cancer.

Though verbally and emotionally victimized by her father, Steven's mother did not suffer his physical or sexual abuse. No, indeed not. A boy was his victim of choice. A little boy's torment sustained him.

211

Susan Drescher died when her son was three years old. That is when the social worker delivered Steven into his grandfather's care. Somehow papers shuffled, time passed, and the child was forgotten. He was lost in the system. Why would anyone be concerned about a young boy fortunate enough to be living in the prestigious home of a successful lawyer with a penchant for order and organization who, outside of work, lived the life of a solitary, unassuming, quiet recluse.

The day of his arrival the young Steven was led by his grandfather down into the basement and into a clean, warm, sparsely furnished room which contained a small, neatly made bed, a brown painted dresser, a solid square table and one spindle backed wooden chair. His grandfather removed the blue trousers, beige shirt and white underwear his grandson was wearing. He even removed his navy socks and running shoes.

"This room is kept very warm, my boy. There is no further need for clothing. However, on occasion you and I will enjoy a good time together. I will dress you in lederhosen and show you a life even greater than the one my father showed me," he promised.

In this manner and in this room Steven lives.

I live inside Steven. I reside deep within his heart. No, no, that is not deep enough. I hide away even deeper within him. I am in his stomach. I sleep in his intestines. Without me Steven is gutless. I am his guts. He created me so that I would protect him from Heinrich. I am doing a hopeless job.

I confess that for nine of Steven's ten years I have stayed hidden. Even though I've been aware of the atrocities taking place since the loss of his mother, I'm ashamed to admit that throughout all these years I have done nothing to help; nothing to save his sanity.

I've been just the listener; the observer of sights I do not want to see.

But this past year, since Steven turned ten years old, I begin to feel more present. I feel myself growing stronger; more confident and more determined to come to his aid.

Neither Steven nor I have been outside this room for seven years. Throughout this time we have listened to Heinrich's explicit oratory; his eloquent but quiet, plain preaching using words not intended for a young boy's listening. When he is not offering oral recitation, Heinrich Drescher has a compulsive tendency to place objects, phallic in appearance, inside his mouth.

He suckles and derives great pleasure knowing he has a watching captive audience. Steven knows no life other than the one he endures. I have memory of his mother but Steven has forgotten that there was a time in his life when someone loved him and had a sincere caring for his well-being.

Sometimes Heinrich will pass the source of his oral delight to his grandson. "Imbibe, my boy," he gently orders with a smile on his face. Steven, to please his captor, does as he is told.

And I distance myself from the sordid exhibition; untouched by the wretched reality. I refuse to be a participant. But I listen.

I listen to his rhythmic voice as he speaks of the memories he has of his own upbringing in Germany. This is how I know that Heinrich Drescher wants to repeat the things he, himself, was taught at an early age by his father. For this reason as Steven matures and grows physically Heinrich use his computer to go online where he purchases the lederhosen; the leather shorts with the H-shaped suspenders that he, himself, wore as a child growing up. As Steven becomes taller his grandfather places his order for a larger size.

I listen to his complimentary words each time he dresses Steven's naked body in the leather costume. In a soft voice he whispers, "How handsome you look, my boy."

One day a few months ago everything changed.

Steven and I are sitting on the edge of the bed when the door to the room is unlocked and opened. Heinrich enters the room. In his right hand he holds a plate containing one of Steven's favourites, a peanut butter and jelly sandwich, while under his arm he carries a brown paper-wrapped parcel. "Your new lederhosen has arrived, my boy!" he announces with quiet glee.

Steven says nothing.

I watch as his grandfather places the sandwich on the square table. "Come, my boy. Sit to the table. You eat and enjoy your lunch while I unwrap the parcel. Or would you like to unwrap it yourself, Steven?"

"No, grandfather, you can do it," Steven answers as he quietly sits and eats his food.

The parcel opened reveals the new brown lederhosen. "These look large," the grandfather says. "Stand, Steven, and let me see if these are going to fit you."

"Don't stand! Stay where you are!" I scream.

I know Steven hears me. He remains sitting, hesitating, unsure what to do.

"I will just finish my sandwich first, sir."

I know I must try harder. I need to be strong enough to allow my voice to come through to the grandfather.

"Don't dilly-dally," he says. "I am excited to dress you in your new apparel."

Steven finishes his sandwich and stands as his grandfather requests. In nakedness his vulnerability has nowhere to hide.

"My, you have grown. You have indeed grown, my boy.

"Refuse! Refuse the bugger!" I yell.

I know Steven hears me. I feel his hesitation. He is still unsure what to do.

I watch as his grandfather lays the lederhosen aside. He opens his mouth wider and kneels before his frightened grandson.

"No," I scream. "No more, you pervert!"

Steven cannot believe my strenuous refusal has come from his voice. I cannot believe it either. And now, for the first time, I am stronger than Steven who is now hiding safely within me. Steve is now in control.

I don't know how this switch has occurred. It is not until after the deed is done that I will first hear the words *dissociative disorder* and the term *multiple personalities*. What I do know is that I will not stand still. I will not be a victim.

"Back off! Get away from me!" I scream.

The grandfather is baffled. "Come, come, my boy," he says. "Haven't we always enjoyed ourselves with the dildo? Think how much more enjoyable it will be for us now that you have grown to be such a big boy?"

"Back off!" I scream again but the power I feel within me is not enough to stop him. Kneeling on the clean floor before me, the grandfather's filth kills the last vestiges of my innocence.

I know Steven can't help me anymore than I'd been able to help him. I cry for help and then I feel the presence of someone inside of me. "Who are you?" I ask in silence.

"You can call me Steph," he replies.

"Can you help me?" I beg.

In response Steph reaches out. I watch as, with my arms, he picks up from the table the string that had wrapped the parcel. As I feel him lower my head to look down upon the head of Steven's grandfather he holds the string outstretched in both hands.

"I can do it," Steph says. "Should I do it?"

"Do it!" I say. And then I am no longer in control.

Steven has returned. To Steph he shouts, "Do it!"

As Steven and I huddle together we simply watch as Steph lowers the string to the back of the grandfather's head. *"Grandfather, look at me,"* he says.

And the grandfather removes his mouth from its helpless target, lifts his head, looks at the boy and says, "Yes, what is it, my boy?"

In that instant Steph pulls the strong string taut. He does not stop pulling until the grandfather collapses on the floor.

"He is dead," Steph declares.

"Are you sure?" Steven asks.

"Yes, he is dead," I confirm.

It is several days before the police make their presence known in the basement. The grandfather's missed attendance at work raises an alarm and at last an investigation commences.

A naked child is found huddled on the floor in a corner of the tidy room.

The grandfather's body, string around its neck, lays sprawled on the floor beside the table in the centre of the room.

I watch as a police officer approaches the boy. "Don't be afraid, son," he says. "What is your name?"

"I don't know," the boy replies.

"Steven, tell him your name is Steve. Let them punish me."

I can hear Steven's sobs. He is hungry, tired and plain scared. He cannot speak.

"Try to remember, son," the police officer says. "What is your name?"

The naked boy looks up into the officer's eyes and I hear him say, "My name is Steph."

Handing him a blanket the officer says, "Here, Steph. Wrap yourself in this."

Both Steven and I listen with admiration as Steph assumes all responsibility for the grandfather's death.

Later in the hospital we both listen as Steph dialogues with the psychiatrist who uses the big words like *dissociative disorder* and *multiple personalities.* He talks about ways in which these personalities can become one.

I am not sure by which name this *one* will be called. Will his name be Steven, Steve or will his name be Steph? I don't know. I know only that at last we are all in a safe place. We are properly clothed and no one is touching anyone in an inappropriate manner.

At this time Steph seems to be the strongest. Steven has been through a lot and for now he chooses to stay hidden. As for me, until the healing process is closer to completion, I am content to remain the second self.

IN THE FOREST

a narrative poem

In the forest deep

Chester weeps;

an angry weeping

sweeping

through the memories

of forgotten days

when her golden tresses

lay like carpet

upon his chest.

Beneath his footsteps

hear the crunch

of purple, yellow, red.

He'd made his bed

they said

when young and foolish;

all was green and life was seen

to be at last like glass,

clear with purpose.

Now leather boots stamp out the pain

but stamp they will without success

like city dwellers trample the roach;

still they encroach

and pain decides

to show no mercy.

Still Chester trods upon the earth

between the trees

beneath the sky

and wonders why

things had to be the way they were;

he'd been so sure.

His Helen was his better half,

his fullness sufficient,

his golden calf sacrificed

but why, dear God?

Why did I create

this hollow emptiness?

What can I do

to make things right?

His questions fall

upon the dirt

where squirrels and chipmunks

play and flirt

heedless of his tramping boots

they climb the trees;

they live with ease

and have no time for Chester's grief.

Memory of the wedding day

when two young hearts

were joined as one

beneath the maple

on edge of woods

where they built their house

to last a hundred years

and more.

Hard he had worked

and so had she

to make this dream reality

and soon a home

was strongly standing

at the edge of a forest

which rose above the coulee

and in this valley

they felt safe.

Chester loved Helen

and she adored him.

They lived carefully

in the valley of marriage,

through the windows of home

viewing a forest

they were fearful to roam.

Oh, my dear,

from whence came the fear?

The house was a strong one

built firmly on rock.

For hours they talked

of what they would do

to foster prosperity,

affluence,

wealth,

and please, dear God,

we will maintain good health.

In love with their house

they filled it with stuff

that all couples wanted.

There was never enough.

The house alone first

filled their desire

but it felt empty now

without couch and gas fire.

They sat by the window

and looked at the forest

but time passing caused them

to think they need curtains

and so they were purchased,

hung from a rod;

the forest was hidden,

even its sod.

Chester worked in a factory

where lamp-stands were made.

Helen worked in a bakery

and all day

they stayed away

from the house they owned.

They filled it with lamps

for which tables were needed

then bought some more chairs

on which to rest.

The forest forgotten

they lived for their house;

many debts to pay

for fluff and stuff

that needed more

to keep itself company.

The bed needed blankets

and the drawers needed clothes.

Back then

they still needed each other

I suppose.

Months became years

and years became heavy.

The youth of their wedding

was declining steady,

as steady,

as sturdy

as rickety stability.

Yet they felt secure

in this unbalanced place.

How one might ask

but not Chester nor Helen.

They never doubted

their methods or ways;

secure in the knowledge

that one of these days

they'd make time to walk

in the forest

again.

Too tired for caressing

and holding and loving;

too tired for dreaming

impossible dreams;

too wrapped up in furniture,

credit cards,

bank loans

Chester and Helen

were suddenly drones.

In the forest

trees listened

and waited with patience.

They knew with a certainty

what was to come

but Chester and Helen

were caught unaware.

They had no idea

what they had done.

They followed the rules and,

yes, they were fools

but fools like their neighbours

who used the same tools

to build what was thought

to be everyone's dream

or so it would seem.

The house was now bulging

with all kinds of stuff

like TV's and paintings,

there was never enough.

Helen grew quiet.

And Chester got rough.

Appliances white

need replacement.

They need to be stainless.

Just work a little harder.

It really is painless.

Who cares if you are working

twelve hour shifts

as long as you can afford

to buy expensive gifts?

And the forest was listening.

It heard the first punch.

It happened while Helen

was making their lunch

to carry to work

the following day.

Chester was sorry,

at least

that's what they say.

The bread it was white

and perhaps a day old.

Baloney was what Helen

planned for the meal.

Hogwash said Chester,

his words angry and terse.

I work all these hours

and deserve something better

like roast beef or chicken;

not baloney or worse.

I'm sorry, said Helen,

it's all that we have.

By the time bills were paid

there was no money left

but I managed baloney

though the budget

was stretched

to its limit and further

than you could guess.

I don't want to hear this,

Chester was screaming.

His arm stretched way back

like a wind blown tree

leaning to touch the ground

he found

violence lurking.

He brought it around

and the sound was whack!

And Helen lay on the floor

of the coulee;

the valley of dread

where no angels tread,

she bled.

On the kitchen floor crying

there was no denying

that Chester had struck

with the force of the devil.

I'm sorry, he cried,

God knows

I don't want to hurt

the only dear woman

I love.

God, please send your

forgiveness

down from above.

They hugged

and they pardoned

and ate the baloney.

And lived the baloney

for several more years

and several more tears

were shed by poor Helen

at the edge of the forest

and Chester grew silent.

In the forest, snow melted

and trees were still barren

yet they stood

majestically proud.

Spring was arriving,

water flowed

through the coulee.

He again was unruly

and violence reined

in the house

filled with stuff

that was never enough.

Through summery days

Helen lived in a daze.

Her job left behind

she prayed he'd be kind

but her prayers

were not answered

that hour.

Whack! Whomp! Kick!

Devour!

Chester sat in the yard

and stared at the trees.

In all of these years

they had lived in the forest

of material greed.

Autumn was approaching,

so too was the fall.

It happened on Monday,

October the twentieth.

Chester beat Helen

in an hour of rage

then set off to work

in the factory of lights

while his heart hid in darkness

ashamed of the fights.

Helen lifted herself

and prayed to the heavens,

packed her suitcase with clothes

and fled to the shelter

where arms opened wide

and her heart filled with hope.

Helen had reached

the end of her rope.

Chester came home

to an empty house

though packed to the rafters

with stuff and fluff.

The house was empty

and Helen was gone.

He was alone

and the hours were long.

In the forest the leaves

had turned purple and red.

The squirrels were collecting

twigs for their bed.

The bears were foraging

needing more food

before winter arrived

and their sleep was good.

Chester sat in the kitchen

upon a smart chair

that had cost even more

than his pay cheque could bear.

And the chair felt hard

and his body was stiff

as the corpse of his marriage

through his mind did drift.

He arose from the chair

and stood by the window,

tore down the drapes

to let in the light.

He looked at the forest

knowing he'd lost the fight.

His only love,

his Helen, was gone.

Finally for her

peacefulness shone.

What have I done?

he asked the trees.

Come to us, they replied,

we offer you peace.

He left the house,

the stuff, the fluff.

He left the coulee

and climbed the hills

into the forest

for rest he searched.

He walked for miles

remembering smiles

that he turned to frowns

when he knocked her down.

Though the forest was tall

and close at hand

Chester and Helen

Could not see the trees.

They did not seek the peace

and protection

resting on the soft earth

beneath the sheltering branches.

In the valley

on a rock

they had built their house.

And in this house

their world was small.

They lived on the edge;

the edge of life;

the edge of sanity;

the edge of the forest.

And now in the forest deep

Chester weeps;

an angry weeping

sweeping

through the memories

of forgotten days

when her golden tresses

lay like carpet

upon his chest.

Beneath his footsteps

hear the crunch of

purple, yellow, red.

He'd made his bed

they said

when young and foolish;

all was green

and life was seen

to be at last

like glass,

·clear with purpose.

ANDREW'S ACHIEVEMENT

"You can't make me do it again!" the old man shouts.

I hear the alarm in his voice. I see the fearful determination in watery blue eyes narrowly set above a nose that shows obvious signs of earlier breakage; a boxer's nose but I know this man has never in all of his eighty-one years participated in the sport of pugilism.

And how do I know this? Because I am beside myself! Not only do I feel beside myself, I'm outside of myself watching the too familiar unfoldment of a scene better viewed by a theatre-goer than from behind the drama playing out at my old scratched-up kitchen table.

"Sign the damn cheque!"

I prefer being detached and don't want to return but I can't bear to watch the old man struggle alone any longer. Back inside my body I immediately feel the pain I had managed to escape for a brief interval, not that it doesn't break my heart and not that it isn't painful to see the old man being abused. But to escape the physical agony of large masculine hands clapping ears as one would a bass drum in a marching band offers some relief.

I find my voice and repeat my vow. "No, Tom, you can't make me do it again!"

A prisoner in my wheelchair I look up at the red-faced, balding, middle-aged man. His long, lean body stretches over the table from where he has planted his feet on the kitchen floor directly across from me. He lifts his right hand from the table top. Like a sparrow in winter I try to puff up my body, hunch my shoulders and pull my head inward to a place of safety in order to escape the full brunt of another smack.

He surprises me this time. He doesn't hit me again. Instead he turns his angry eyes away from me and looks down at the Rolex on his wrist.

"Shit! I have to get to work old man but when I get home tonight I want to see that signed cheque on the table! You understand me?"

I give him my silent response.

His voice raises another octave but he's not shouting yet. "I said do you understand me, old man?"

"You can't make me!" I whisper.

Whack!

My head rolls atop my neck which suddenly feels like a slinky toy. Grateful for the shoulder upon which my right ear rests I raise my left hand to soothe and cover the biting pain reverberating in and around my left eye.

This slanted one-eyed perspective of the perpetrator, though clear, is impossible to accept. He looks like Tom but where is the little boy who stood in uniform with his pack and recited, *"On my honour I promise to do my duty to God and the Queen; to do my best to help others whatever it costs me and to obey the Scout Law."*

I want to remember the baseball games, the picnics, the ice-fishing and the ordinary, camaraderie; the mutual trust and friendship we shared throughout Tom's growing up years. I want to remember these things but it's not easy. My ears are ringing and the stinging pain around my left eye leaves me feeling powerless.

Yes, as I crouch in my chair, I feel helpless but at the same time I know that somehow I must bear the responsibility for what is going on in my home. I don't know where I went wrong but it must be my fault. After all, I raised the boy though I swear I rarely raised my voice and I never laid a hand on him.

As a father my heart bursts with pride the day Tom graduates with honours from high school. Friends can't stop me bragging about my son's remarkable academic achievements in university. I didn't even graduate from high school myself and as I stand beside his mother offering applause the day he receives his Master's Degree it is all I can do to restrain my emotions and keep the joyful tears that fall freely from his mother's eyes hidden behind my own.

Today I don't feel proud to acknowledge that Tom is my son. I thank God his mother is not here to see what is going on. The violence lurking inside his hardened heart doesn't creep out of the closet and present itself to me until several weeks after the day of my Stella's funeral. I'm glad she is dead and buried. I hope and pray she can't see what is happening from wherever she is in her spiritual home. If Stella were alive today the overwhelming sense of disbelief and shame would kill her.

I hear the door slam. Tom is on his way to work and I know he won't be back until after six this evening. I don't know exactly when my only son became the victim of a gambling addiction. I don't know how or why it happened. He had everything going for him.

Soon after his graduation from university he is hired by one of the largest corporate entities in Canada, George Weston Limited. Now before Tom started working there, the only thing I knew about Weston's was that my mother used to buy their bread and cakes when the bread man made his daily visits selling Weston's wares to my childhood home.

Within ten years of his graduation Tom is one of the highly-paid top executives in the company. Though I never know the price of the ticket I know he makes big bucks. During these years Tom meets Alice and I will never forget how happy and proud Stella and I are on our son's wedding day.   Tom and Alice never had any children. I never fully understand what happened to end what I think is an idyllic marriage.

I do question Tom about it but all he ever said was, "Money problems."

I want to ask him why, when he is earning such a high income, he has money problems but Stella tells me I am best to mind my own business and stay out of it. That's exactly what I do.

Within a year or two of Tom's divorce from Alice he begins coming around the house wanting to borrow money from me. I do okay throughout the years working at the steel plant. I never make big bucks like my son but the union takes care of its own. My wife works as a clerk typist in the same steel plant. Together we do okay. Stella and I buy this nice little house and I am always able to drive a good car. It is not always easy but we live carefully and save the money that carries Tom throughout his years away from home getting that fine education.

Everything changes for Stella and me when I get sick. The doctor calls it peripheral artery disease; something I'd never heard of before but this is what I have and I'm told it is in my legs. When I ask the doctor for an explanation he tells me a more common name for the disease is *hardening of the arteries*; the same arteries that are supposed to supply blood to my legs and feet.

When I start to notice the symptoms I don't pay a lot of attention because I think the achiness in my legs and the discomfort in my feet is just a result of standing on the concrete floor in the steel plant day in and day out for many long years. I don't know then that my addiction to tobacco is putting me at a higher risk and when the doctor diagnoses high blood pressure I just put that down to the stress of working long hours to pay off the mortgage and keep the house running because by this time in my life Stella is already very sick and no longer able to work.

They tell me Stella has lung cancer. In less than a year from the time of her diagnosis the Good Lord takes Stella home.

I live in my little house alone after that. I miss my wife. At night when I lay alone in my bed I have painful cramps in my legs that keep me awake so that in the morning I always feel groggy when I set off for work. The doctor tells me to quit smoking but to me, it is like the only pleasure I have in life. I don't pay any attention to his advice until I begin to develop painful, black, non-bleeding ulcers on my feet. Then the doctor tells me if I don't stop smoking I could lose my legs one day.

Guess that's what I needed to hear because, although it isn't easy, I quit smoking and haven't had a cigarette since. I try to take care of my feet the way the doctor explained that I should and though I don't consciously try to lose weight, once I lose my Stella, the pounds start dropping off me. I never did know how to cook a decent meal. Doctor tells me my cholesterol is off the scales and that I should be eating healthy on a regular basis. I never tell him my suppers consist of Hungry Man Dinners or Big Macs most nights.

The doctor prescribes pain meds and meds to lower my cholesterol and meds to prevent blood from forming clots in my arteries. He is trying to be my best friend but after Stella's death I don't have the same interest in life as I did when we were together. It isn't intentional but in many ways I become my worst enemy following an unhealthy lifestyle and I am losing more and more time off work. At last I have no choice but to give up working and go on disability.

I develop ugly open sores on my lower legs and the day comes when the doctor tells me my only option is surgery. I am going to lose both legs and be confined to a wheelchair.

These are very stressful years with the death of my wife; my son's divorce and the amputation of my legs. I don't think my life can get any worse than it is.

Throughout all this time my son, Tom, visits me. And at first I welcome him with open arms. They are real visits where we sit together, have a beer, and talk about whatever comes into our heads to talk about.

But in time this changes too. It seems Tom is always short of money. "It's the high cost of lawyers for this divorce," he explains in the beginning. To me, that is understandable and I don't object to giving him a few dollars whenever I can. I don't find that too big a challenge during the years I am working at the steel plant and bringing home a good pay cheque. I am mortgage-free by the time I am forced to quit work and go onto disability so I can manage financially and I feel I can afford to lend him a few dollars here and there whenever he asks.

I miss my Stella and I miss my buddies at work. I feel trapped in my chair and I'm becoming something I never thought I could be; a lonely old man. For this reason I feel I really need Tom's visits and if they cost me a few bucks so be it. Just having his company makes the expense acceptable. Guess you could say I am buying his time.

But in the last few years Tom's requests are becoming more like demands.

I say to him, "Tom, your divorce is long over and paid for. You've got nobody to look after but yourself. You've got a good, high paying job and here you are asking your old man for money. What's the story? What's going on, son?"

That's when Tom breaks down. He sits at my old scratched up kitchen table and bawls his eyes out like he is a little kid or an old woman. "What's the matter, Tom? Tell me what's happening to upset you this way."

That's when he confesses to me. He tells me all about his trips to casinos, the private card games, the horses, and all the bets on all the sports games.

After that day I start my own investigation and I learn about an organization something like Alcoholics Anonymous but called Gamblers Anonymous.

Tom actually thanks me for my help at that time. I give him all the information I have gathered and he says, "I promise, Dad, I'll go to the meetings. But in the meantime can you loan me five hundred. I'm way short of my apartment rental and facing eviction.

As I write him the cheque for five hundred dollars, I say, "Tom, with your Mother gone this house is too big for an old guy like me. Why not give up your apartment, move in here with me. I can manage the rent and that will give you some extra to get your gambling debts paid off."

"Thanks, Dad," he exclaims.

And that is how it came to be that Tom lives with me in my house. How did it come to be that the loving son went from saying, *thanks Dad* to demanding, *sign the damn cheque?* I don't know. It is a gradual process leading up to today where I sit in my wheelchair nursing my injured ears and doing my best to soothe the pain in my left eye.

I know I need help. I know I have my legal rights. This is still my house, bought and paid for. The little money I have is my money and it is hard enough to support myself on a disability cheque never mind putting food on the table for Tom who never brings a penny into the house. Taking! Always wanting, demanding and always getting what he wants. Always I end up signing the damn cheque.

Today I know this has to stop. In the first place I'm running out of money. My bank account is almost running on empty. In the second place I am sick to death of being my son's punching bag.

I have only a few hours before Tom's return to my place. I make up my mind. I had told him, "You can't make me do it again!" This time I mean exactly what I have said. Clapping my ears the way he did today is the last straw!

I wheel myself to the phone and get busy making some appointments. I make an appointment at the local community legal clinic. I talk on the phone with our town's Senior Issues Officer and after talking to him I put in a call to a locksmith. Within an hour he is there putting new locks on my doors.

Although I hate to let anyone in on the shame I feel I know it is time to stop keeping what the Senior Issues Officer calls *elder abuse* a secret. So I call one of my work buddies. Bill lives only a few blocks away. It isn't easy to talk about what is going on but I've known Bill for a lot of years. I confide in him and he doesn't mock me. He doesn't tell me I've been stupid. He doesn't ask me why I've put up with that kind of shit! He doesn't hang up on me. What he does say is, "I'm on my way over."

Within twenty minutes Bill is knocking on my door. He is a widower too, living alone, and on this day he looks at my bruised eye and says, "I've brought my suitcase. Where's the guest room? I'm planning to stay for a while.

When Tom arrives home this evening he is greeted at the door by two police officers. He is charged with *elder abuse.*

Tom is not receptive or cooperative with the arresting officers. He tries to punch one of the cops. Just before they cuff him Tom lifts his right hand and raising his middle finger he spits at me.

My heart is broken. My son, the brilliant achiever and my reason for living, is giving me the finger. I don't want to see it. Instead I remember my young son in his Boy Scout uniform giving me the three-fingered Scout sign and promising, *I will do my best to help others.*

It is not an easy thing to call the police on your own son but it is something I finally know I have to do. I recognize that for too many years I enabled his addiction. In the beginning I refuse but in the end I always relent and write out a cheque when he demands I give him money. I don't like to admit the fact that I am afraid of my son. I am grateful that from somewhere I find courage and on this day I refuse to allow one more day of my life to be ruled by fear.

My name is Andrew. I'm an old man and I haven't accomplished a whole lot with my life. But I always worked hard to the best of my ability and I provided a stable, caring home for my wife, Stella, and my son, Tom.

For several years since the death of my wife I allowed myself to become an enabler and a victim. On that life-changing day, at last, I stood up for myself. I can look at my face in a mirror now and feel like a man again. I stood up and I said no. I meant what I said and, though it may not seem like much to some; to me, finding the courage to say no is my greatest life achievement.

Author's Bio:

Audrey Austin was born and raised by her parents in Toronto, Ontario, Canada. At an early age she married and before long her two daughters arrived. Having only a high school education she waited until her children were grown before going back to school. She attended University of Toronto and later graduated from Transformational Arts College. She has lived in Toronto & its suburbs; Prince Edward Island and in New Zealand. She has enjoyed other international travel but only as a tourist in countries such as Thailand; Korea; Bahamas; Bermuda; Columbia, Puno and Cartagena in South America. She always wanted to write and did so in a small way as a hobby but never made any attempt at publication. It was not until she retired at an uncertain age that she finally made the promise to herself that she would fulfill her dream of being an author. She loves creative writing and how can something one loves so much be classified as work? She has written novels, novellas, and short stories always doing her best to keep up with the characters. Audrey is currently living in Elliot Lake, Ontario, Canada.

http://www.amazon.com/author/audreyaustin

http://www.facebook.com/audreyaustinca

www.ingramcontent.com/pod-product-compliance
Lightning Source LLC
Chambersburg PA
CBHW051146030726
47504CB00004B/1073